The Talisman S

Riders of

Fire and Ice

Brett Salter

TO MY BEST FRIEND/BROTHER
BRIAN FLANAGAN. NOT FOR ANY
REASON IN PARTICULAR. HE IS
JUST REALLY COOL.

Special thanks to Michael Lubin for his

amazing artwork and Micki and Daryl

Watkins for their diligent editing skills

Riders of Fire and Ice

"Into eternal darkness, into fire and into ice."— DANTE ALIGHIERI

Prologue

First, a short history lesson.

(For those of you who have read book one, you can skip this part. For those of you coming late to the party, you probably need this.)

Long ago, before mankind held any power, the Earth was quite different. It was a dark and evil realm. Inhabiting the shadows were several races of creatures that were known as the Darkbrands. These malevolent brutes were united under the rule of a cruel and despicable warlord known as The Tyrant King.

At the same time, living in the mountains, was a resilient race of beings, the Dens of the Dragons. The First, the original dragon lord, was the leader of the Dragon Dens. The Tyrant King wanted to destroy the dragons because they offered harmony to the chaos of the world. The First possessed much of the same ambition and sought domination as well. His desire was to eradicate the Darkbrands and to claim the entire realm for himself. Under the guise of a peace treaty, a ritual was created to unite the two wicked lords' hearts thus giving the possibility of control to ONE leader. You see, all dragons, even The First, are born with incomplete hearts. No dragon could ever reach his full potential unless bonded with another entity, but the Tyrant King did not know this. The Tyrant King and The First could not wait to gain control over the other and become the solitary ruler of Earth.

During the ritual, a strange and beautiful thing happened. The evil that was in The First's heart was released. As The First's new heart became pure with the magic, The Tyrant King's heart became ever darker. In the next few years, he put his plan to enslave the dragons into motion. But the power of The First was too great. He and his dragons destroyed much of The Tyrant King's army. Since The First and The Tyrant King shared the same heart, the dragon realized he could not kill his bound brother. The First knew he would need to detain The Tyrant King, so he banished him and his minions to The Void a realm created from the evil that left The First's heart.

As peace and goodness flourished in the world, the race of man began to rise. In the early years, the dragons fought many wars against the evil that slips into our world from The Void. It wasn't until the time of King Arthur that the Great Synergy was revived and men and dragons found that together they could protect the realm of Earth. But men were not as pure of heart as dragons, and as time lengthened the distance from Arthur and his knights, men became distrustful of dragons. Not willing to fight against this race they grew to love, the dragons simply used their innate magic and disappeared. That was until the evil of The Void began to leak in earnest into our world again.

Now, let's take some time to catch you up with our two unwitting heroes from the first book. You know, before delving into their epic feats and slipups in this one.

Rome Lockheed and Julian Rider are two middle school kids that share a secret. Rome is really a fire dragon from the Den of Volcana trapped in a boy's body. Weird, right? Julian, his blood-brother, uses his magically imbued die to change Rome into the dragon and himself into a weapon-wielding, armor-clad Synergist Knight. Cool, right? The local librarian, Mr. Jones, has been training them to harness these powers and use them to defend the Earth against waves of invading monsters called Darkbrands from an alternate dimension. Creepy, right?

So far, they are three for three in these random encounters, but their victories have drawn the attention of someone or something residing in the shadows. The mystery figure's identity has not been revealed, but you have a pretty good idea who it is by now, don't you? We catch up with the boys on their way to England to find more portals to seal and more allies to join their cause. Who knows what else they'll find or what will find them in the ancient stomping grounds of Camelot.

Chapter One

Rome hadn't even set foot on the plane and Julian was already making plenty of complaining comments. "We don't need to fly in a plane, dude," he said. "We have our own mode of transportation with you! We don't need a runway, or a pilot, or even an in-flight movie! I mean, with you being a dragon, there is no possible situation where we will ever even need a car! Ever! You hear me? Ever!"

"Yeah," said Rome. "But where would you put your luggage? I am not hauling a semester's worth of clothes on my back across the Atlantic Ocean for you. And how would we explain how we got all the way to England when NONE of our classmates saw us on the plane. Or you know who?"

"Oh, yeah," soured Julian. "I forgot about her." Julian glared across the terminal at the "who" that Rome was referring to.

Mrs. Case was the boys' principal at Dampier Middle School where they went to get their public education in Canton, Georgia. She was a very friendly educator who got along well with her students and faculty. She was young and full of fresh ideas that made her popular among her peers as well. It was said that she had a hypnotic way about her. Everyone felt compelled to tell her whatever she wanted to know. For reasons only known to them, Rome and Julian did not trust her. The fact that she said she would be watching them really agitated Rome. It was as if she knew something about their secret, but did not want them to know that she knew. And Julian just did not really like authority figures or any kind of administrative presence.

What was the secret that the boys carried with them to England? It was the fact that Rome was really a thirty-foot, fire-breathing dragon who had made an ancient pact with Julian. By using a family heirloom given to Julian, the duo had bonded their hearts forever and opened up powers hidden from the world for several centuries. Together, they were destined to fight against an army of shadow creatures constantly threatening to take over their world. Pretty run of the mill secret, right?

Besides the boys, only one other knew the real reasons for their voyage to England. Mr. Jones, who was their trusted librarian/guardian had sent them there to find out more about the underground movements of their enemies. The three of them figured that since the original Despot War had taken place in Britannia during the days of Camelot, there would be plenty of clues to follow up on and cryptic stones to overturn. To their knowledge, they were the only three who knew the trip's true meaning. Of course, in time, they would find that to be false as well.

During the previous month, the boys had successfully sealed a portal to The Void where the vile Darkbrands were coming through to scout the Earth for their master. Apparently, there were many of these portals around the world. Mr. Jones, Rome, and Julian had made it their mission to close as many of these portals as they could. Crowning themselves as Earth's new defenders, they challenged themselves to become a revolution against the Darkbrand army and the will of The Tyrant King. However, they were going to need help.

That was the second reason for their journey to England. Mr. Jones assured them that there were other "players" with knowledge about the impending war like Julian's father. You see, Julian came from a long line of knights sworn to protect the Earth from the "baddies" of The Void, but they did NOT believe in keeping dragons as allies like the knights of Camelot did. Julian, not being a big fan of authority, had strayed from his father's teaching and performed The Great Synergy (or something close to it) with Rome. Thanks to Julian's mysterious die artifact, they now shared a lifetime bond between them that provided them with formidable powers. The Great Synergy was frowned upon by Julian's family, so they kept that a secret too.

In line with Julian's upstart tendencies, the boys chose to travel to England to seek out any allies they may come across. Unbeknownst to Mr. Rider, he was footing the bill for the boys' expedition. It was a two pronged assignment, and the boys were terribly excited to carry it out to a successful conclusion.

There were a couple drawbacks to this undertaking though. The first was that Mrs. Case, the unrelenting enigma, was joining them as a chaperone. The second was that while the boys were in Somerset County, they would have to visit Julian's little sister who attended the boarding school right there in Bridgewater. Rome had never met her, but he had heard stories about her from

Julian for the last three weeks.

"She's just the most annoying little pest ever!" he said reading Rome's thoughts. "She's soooooo frustrating to deal with. She's always mimicking me and trying to one up me around my parents. I would rather be strapped to a bed and forced to watch Disney movies for a week than have to be around her for one day. Once, she put a tack on my chair in front of my dad so that I would lose my cool on her and break my knightly persona. She's always trying to expose me or narc me out. That little brat booger!" Julian kept going, but Rome put in his earplugs and settled into his seat. Camela Rider sounded like a handful.

Rome had never been happier to be an only dragonling. If little sister humans were this bad, he was sure little sister dragons had to be ten times worse. Rome could imagine a miniature version of himself always getting on his nerves and breathing flames at his baseball card collection. Earlier in the week, Rome had jokingly promised Julian that if Camela got on their nerves too much, he would shoot fire at her feet and make her dance until she passed out from exhaustion. Julian had demanded more. Rome would do anything for his blood brother, but he would not use his dragon powers to harm the innocent. Julian had retorted that Camela was about as innocent as a snake. Rome had frowned doubtfully.

The boys chatted between themselves for most of the flight. It was a little over eight hours to arrive in Bridgewater, England where the boys would be staying. As fate would have it, their trip took them right to the county of Somerset where Camelot was said to have flourished nearly one thousand years ago. Rome thought maybe it was more than just coincidence. His idea was that some higher powers had made this trip a reality. Rome was not sure whether to fear or welcome whoever orchestrated this, but he was resolute in finding out one way or another.

At least ten times during the flight Rome glanced up to catch Mrs. Case staring at him. Every time she would quickly turn her head away as if it had been unintentional, but Rome could feel her eyes upon him. Why did she watch him all the time? What did she know? Mr. Jones had warned the boys about outside influences. Could she be a possible ally for the boys in their fight against the Darkbrands?

Rome decided to fire up the spatial linking which was one of the abilities they shared after performing The Great Synergy. It allowed them to talk to each other telepathically. It was really helpful for keeping the uninvited out of private conversations.

"Should we ask Mrs. Case if she knows about what we are doing'" Rome asked Julian over their spatial linking. "I mean, it is quite obvious she knows something. Maybe she can help us."

Julian cackled louder than the engines. "C'mon, dude," he bellowed back across the spatial linking. "She might think we are up to something, but there's no way she knows the truth about us. Think about it. If she were a friend, she would have reached out to us by now. If she were an enemy, she would have attacked us like those mindless Garms we eradicated. She's just very concerned with her students' behavior. I mean, it IS a little disturbing to her that we were there when the whole main hall got absolutely obliterated. She's probably just concerned we are in a gang or something."

Rome broke off the spatial linking and let his eyes turn red. "I do not trust her," he snarled. "Mr. Jones warned us to stay alert. She wants to watch us? I will be watching her too!" He turned to face her, and once again she shot a look back at him and smiled.

"Just quit making us look obvious," pleaded Julian. "The last thing we need while we're here is to get put on suspension or detention or any other "tion". That would surely limit the time we have for research, man."

Rome sat up straight in his seat. "What IS the plan for when we get there?" he asked. "We have absolutely no leads to go on. Are we just supposed to go sit out in the woods and wait for monsters to show up?"

Julian threw himself back into his seat and crossed his arms. "Relax, Rome," he said. "I've got it all figured out. We'll go see my sister. As much of a pain as she is, she is still from the House of Rider. She is aware of the whole situation our realm faces. She may already have some good leads for us. Besides, I haven't seen her since she got shipped off to England last summer. Maybe she's changed."

Rome wondered to himself how bad Julian's sister could possibly be. Was she worse than the Garms they had fought in the woods? Rome seriously doubted that.

Suddenly Julian jumped up in his seat. "What if she's gotten worse than when she left," he asked to the open air. He slowly and comically reached for the "barf bag" on the seat in front of him.

Rome smiled widely. Julian was quite a handful. The idea of having to deal with two siblings from the House of Rider sounded both excruciating and stressful. Rome looked out his window at the giant ocean beneath him. The beautiful colors put him slightly at ease. He wanted to fly again. He wanted to soar into the clouds and feel the winds change directions as he banked into and out of them. His dreams had been filled with montages of all the new exciting things taking place around him recently. His eyes had finally been opened to what his life truly was. He was a dragon. He was a Darkbrand slayer. He was a defender of Earth. His life would never be the same again.

Chapter Two

The plane landed at Bristol Airport in Somerset, England at approximately 11:31 A.M. That gave the boys enough time to make it to Bridgewater and meet with Camela when she would be finishing up classes for the day. Julian said that they would get all their things settled in at the dormitories with the rest of their fellow students and head over to see his sister in the early evening.

Rome was excited to be in a new country. He had never even been north of the Mason-Dixon line or west of the Mississippi River. Here he was in Great Britain on a mission to stop a worldwide raid of wicked beings from another dimension. Much to his dismay, it turned out that Bridgewater was much like his hometown of Canton, Georgia. It had rolling hills that spread out like green blankets covering the topography. Wooded patches sprung up from the myriads of sprawling meadows and pastures that blocked the rustic town in on all sides. Rome doubted that much commercialization had touched here since the times of King Arthur's court. Maybe they kept it that way on purpose.

Even the airport located outside of the city was small and quaint. Rome could appreciate an airport that lacked hustle and bustle. It was probably the dragon in him, but he liked the idea of the peaceful countryside away from the city. The area in Somerset County seemed right up Rome's alley.

The boys and their classmates took a double decker bus to downtown Bridgewater where they would be staying for the next three months. The town itself was not small by any means. The downtown area covered about fifteen square miles and was home to a thriving epicenter surrounded by shops and eateries of all varieties. Rome thought that tourism was probably the town's main source of income. He thought to himself that he better not get caught in his true form by any local law enforcement. He could see himself quickly become the center of a freak show charging astronomical prices for tourists around the world to come see a monstrous dragon in the flesh (or diamond hard, blood-red scales in Rome's case).

It turned out that the dormitories provided for the exchange students were the same dormitories that Camela's school used. The local educator met the children out front and gave them a brief history about the buildings which though they looked quite old-fashioned were actually recently renovated. In fact, the wing where Rome and his classmates were staying was only five years old. Perhaps the town's main income came from a foreign exchange program instead of tourism. Rome's mind started wandering about England's per capita and its main exports, when he noticed Mrs. Case had moved close to him.

"It's dark," she breathed harshly. "This whole town has quite a secretive and enchanting past. It's been passed down as legend through oral tradition. You won't find it in any history books, but long ago a very bloody battle took place here and the surrounding area. "

Rome spun around to face her. "How do you know that?" he asked sharply.

"This may be hard for you to understand, Rome," she responded. "But I witnessed the battle from atop those hills to the South." She looked down at him and smiled strangely. "It WILL happen again. History is forever cyclical. Mistakes are doomed to always repeat themselves."

She tapped Rome on the shoulder which made him jump slightly. "If you'll excuse me," she said. "I am going to retreat to my room and unpack. This evening and the next days will surely be full of exciting and peculiar discoveries. I suggest all you kids do the same."

With that she moved to the center of the group and began giving out instructions to each student to help them locate their sleeping quarters. Rome shivered and ground his teeth. What could she possibly mean by that? She was HERE when a battle took place? Surely she meant a dream. Mrs. Case had now officially given Rome the creeps.

Rome was thinking about how uncomfortable the next three months were going to be when he noticed another person moving in close to him. He was both surprised and delighted to see Cecilia Parker standing next to him.

Cecilia was what Rome considered to be a beautiful girl. She wasn't tall, but she wasn't short either. She had flower-scented, red hair that came down past her shoulders. Her shoulders and arms had some signature freckles that came out only at certain times of the year. Rome really liked her freckles. She had a smile that lit up a room, and the most beautiful, steel-blue eyes that ensnared Rome's full attention. As if that weren't enough, she was one of the nicest people Rome had ever met. Life was good when Cecilia Parker was near.

"Hey, Rome," she started. "Can you do me a favor?"

"Sure, Cecilia," said Rome captivated once more by her eyes.

"Would it be okay if I walked to the dorms with you? My roommate Jamie got sick on the plane and had to go to the school nurse for treatment." She laughed which sounded like music. "Oops," she said covering her mouth. "I shouldn't laugh. It's just that I told her before we left to sleep during the flight, but she didn't listen to me. I even gave her some Dramamine."

Rome was so entranced he could barely make out what she was saying, but some primitive instinct in his body took hold and he reached out for Cecilia's suitcase. "Uh, yeah. That is an awfully awful situation," he stammered. "It's just awful. I'm sure she will be fine in a few hours." He giggled uncomfortably. "Ummm. Can I carry your suitcase for you? I love you. I mean, I'd love to HELP you."

Cecilia smiled appreciatively. "That would be so gentlemanly of you. Thanks Rome. Who says chivalry is dead?" Rome could not help but think of Julian and how unscrupulous and crass he was. He decided not to answer her question.

Rome grabbed her suitcase, and the two headed up the front stairs to the lobby. Rome could see out of his right eye that Julian was doubling over in laughter. Rome remembered that he and his brother shared so many things on so many levels through their bond. Julian must have sensed the entire conversation.

Great, thought Rome. Julian was probably never going to let him live that one down. Oh well. If the teasing got too bad, Rome would just sling Julian around with his tail for a while. That made Rome smile.

Rome and Cecilia walked through the lobby and into the elevator. The building was three stories high, but only the second floor was in use by the American students. To keep the boys and girls separated, the powers that be decided to put boys on the left wing and girls on the right. The dorms housed two students per room, but the chaperones got to have their own rooms. For consistency, the female educators would watch the girl's hall, and the male chaperones would watch the boy's hall. Rome was thankful that Mrs. Case would be far away from him when he slept.

Rome walked Cecilia to her room and handed over her suitcase. She thanked him for his assistance, and they talked for a few moments about how exciting it was to be in a foreign country. They shared how neither of them had ever traveled far from home and how cool it would be to experience an education away from their parents. When the banter was over, Rome sauntered to his room on the other side of the building.

When Rome got to his room, the door was wide open. He walked in to see his roommate Julian laying on the floor with his feet pressed up against the wall. He was tossing his die up at the wall and catching it in his hand before it could hit the ground. There were a couple twigs and paperclips strewn around from where Julian had accidentally missed his catch. When he noticed Rome entering the room he jumped up to greet him.

"Hey there partner," he said. "Hurry up and unpack, man. We gotta go meet Camela in the next thirty minutes because she has ballet practice at four o'clock sharp. Unless you want me to go by myself, and you can stay here drooling over Cecilia Parker some more."

Rome frowned at Julian. He threw his suitcase onto his bed and started to unzip it. Then, he paused and looked over his shoulder at Julian. "Hey, Jules. Remind me to tell you what Mrs. Case said to me after we meet your sister," said Rome.

Julian approached Rome and cupped him on the shoulder. "No need," he said. "I sensed the whole thing. Our bond has grown so much in the last month. We can actually share the same experiences now. It's crazy cool!"

"What do you think she meant by that, Jules?" Rome asked.

"I guess she believes in reincarnation, or something," replied Julian. "I mean, Mrs. Case is old, but there's no way she's nine hundred years old, dude! She couldn't possibly have been here when the battle took place. What worries me is that she knew about it. She must be more informed than we thought."

"Mr. Jones told us to be on our toes for anything out of the ordinary," said Rome. "Would you agree that her comments were pretty out of the ordinary?"

"I would definitely say everything about Mrs. Case is pretty out of the ordinary," said Julian. "We should totally follow her at some point and look for any strange tendencies. But before we go down THAT bizarre rabbit hole, let's go meet my darling, little sister." Julian glanced at Rome's open suitcase. "You might want to bring those ear plugs."

Chapter Three

Camela's dormitory was in a different building from where the boys were staying, and, luckily, it was within short walking distance. In fact, it took less than five minutes to walk from THEIR lobby to the lobby entrance of her building. The whole place was shaped like a large rectangle with three stories of student living spaces similar to the where the exchange students were residing.

As the boys walked in the front double doors, they noticed how lively this section was. There were students hanging out all over the lobby chatting, studying, and even playing hackey-sack in the nearby covered area. Rome was beyond pleased to see that his favorite sport was internationally prevalent. Maybe he would have no trouble fitting in with the crowd from overseas.

Julian started walking with purpose to a robust leather chair in one of the side rooms of the common area. Its back was facing the boys as they approached it, but it was obvious someone was sitting in the chair. Julian grabbed the corner of the backrest and swiveled it around to face him.

There sat Camela with her face buried in a book. All Rome could see were her two bright, blonde pigtails popping out the sides of the massive tome she held up to her face. The pigtails themselves were held together by pink and purple hair ties dotted with fake, silver rhinestones. The novel that enveloped her was "The Art of War" by Sun Tzu, and it was comically too large for her tiny hands. She wore what appeared to be a school uniform dress combo with stockings and bantam, black shoes. She did not remove the book when she finally addressed the boys.

"Tis the foul smell of a malodorous brother who seems to have forgotten to brush his teeth again that I smell before me," she said in the squeakiest voice Rome had ever heard. "It is a wonder you remember your own foolish head wherever thou travels take you, Julian. One could say you require daily reminders for fitting your appendages in the appropriate clothes holes and tying your boot straps so as not to fall on your horrible face."

"Oh, shut it, Camela!" yelled Julian. "Could you once be happy to see me without throwing a bunch of insults at me?" Julian breathed into his hand to check his breath.

"It is the fool who brings insults upon himself for he is only a fool and nothing more," she replied coyly.

She moved the book to the side displaying the face of a young girl with wide eyes and a button nose. Rome could easily detect that she was related to Julian. Save for their age difference, their faces were almost carbon copies of each other from the contours of their jawlines to the azure color of their eyes. The Rider family genes were certainly consistent!

Camela continued to tease her brother. "Would you see anything other than a fool should I hold a mirror up to your befuddled expression?"

"That's it," exclaimed Julian. "I don't even know what you are saying, but I know it's making me mad!" He launched at his little sister with his hand wide open intent on smacking her on her right between her pigtails.

Milliseconds before his palm landed squarely on her scalp, it froze in mid-air strangled by the firm grip of another girl who flashed onto the scene out of nowhere. She had intercepted Julian's wrist and held it inches away from Camela's forehead. In one fluid movement, the girl twisted Julian's hand to his outside, side stepped his body, and slung him down to the ground with a thud.

Julian scrambled to get back to his feet and popped up next to Rome ringing his wrist in pain. "Yeeeouch!" he proclaimed. "What was that for?" Julian pointed angrily at the girl and stomped his foot in frustration.

The girl stood next to the chair where Camela sat, and she posed like a Karate combatant. She was average height, but towered over the dainty Camela. Her body was lithe and athletically built, and she was naturally pretty wearing minimal makeup. She had platinum, blonde hair down to her waist that appeared to turn white as you approached the tips. Uncannily, it moved and flowed even though the boys felt no breeze in their direct vicinity. Her eyes were an icy blue that matched her nail polish, and her dangling earrings looked like alabaster snowflakes. She wore the same uniform as Camela, but had brilliant blue shoes and a turquoise sash across her torso. Rome thought her quite striking as she turned sideways

31

to lean against Camela's chair and smirked slightly.

"What are you smirking at?" asked Julian. "That's MY thing."

Camela interjected and laced her fingers. "Most vile brother, allow me to introduce you to my personal bodyguard, consigliere, and friend. This is Krysta Valanche of the eighth grade." She turned her head to face Krysta. "Krysta, meet the reason for my many frustrations and the bane of my existence Julian Pellinore Rider." She made a stink face at him.

"Well, Krysta," Julian started. "You nearly broke my wrist with that judo move or whatever it was. I was just going to pat my little sister on her head. I oughtta kick you right in the shins for that!"

"My apologies, Sir Julian," said Krysta very calmly. "But regardless of your relation, objective, or intention, no one may lay even a finger on Lady Camela. I am sworn to her protection, supervision, and security for all hours of the day." She glanced down at his hand. "Your injury, though painful for now, is not a serious one, and it will heal in short time, Sir."

Julian paced in front of Rome still gripping

his sore wrist. "Well.....okay then. At least I know my sister is in good hands. Whatever." He paused. "It's nice to meet you Krysta." He went to shake her hand, but then pulled back timidly. "I'm glad my little sister has made some friends. We used to have to bribe her classmates to come over for playdates when she was younger."

"Aha!" cackled Camela. "One can always rely on the dimwitted Rider child to cast aspersions out of reactionary anger. Your slander is mere dribble by all my counts." She overlooked him and focused on Rome as if noticing him for the first time. "And who is this who shadows you, brother?"

"Oh yeah. Sorry," fumbled Julian. "Krysta Valanche and Camela Lynette Rider, please meet Rome Lockheed. He's my....uh...well.... he's my friend from back home." Julian stepped aside so Rome could shake hands with the girls.

Camela stood up from her chair and extended her hand out bent at the wrist as if Rome should kiss the back of it. Rome took it and shook it awkwardly. She pulled her hand away and sat back down on her throne huffing as she did so. Under her breath she mumbled something along the lines of "uncouth vermin". Krysta quickly stepped in front of Rome before he could react to the diminutive diva. She smiled at him with wide eyes and flipped her hair.

"It is my sincere pleasure to meet you, Rome Lockheed," she said. "May I say that you have very kind, genuine, and handsome eyes? In fact, most of you is quite handsome." She immediately put her hand to her mouth and her face turned a deep shade of red. "I'm sorry. I didn't mean to be so forward."

Rome laughed. "No problem," he said. "It is very nice to meet you too, Krysta. I like your uniform."

"Oh, we ALL have to wear them," Krysta laughed nervously. "To be truthful, they are quite annoying, bothersome, and uncool." She smiled wistfully at Rome and gave out a quiet sigh. She stared at him for a couple seconds before Julian interrupted the silence.

Julian waved his throbbing hand in front of Krysta's eyes to break off her stare. "Okaaaaaaaay," he said. "So we wanted to meet with Camela to discuss some things. Is there somewhere we could go to talk? Somewhere private?"

"Of course, you phlegm," snapped Camela. "Let us travel to the school's library." She looked at the other students swarming around them. "We will accomplish more towards to your task away from this ruckus."

The boys followed Camela and Krysta down the main hall of the dormitory until it branched off into a smaller hallway. The four of them made small talk about the boys' trip to England and how the time change would affect them more drastically tomorrow than today. Rome picked up on how dissimilar the two girls were. Krysta rarely talked, and Camela could hardly shut up for more than a few seconds. Krysta moved deliberately wasting little energy, while Camela bounced all over the place like a hyperactive Chihuahua. Krysta spoke informally, while Camela used the knight speak that her father and brother (sometimes) demonstrated. Although the girls were very different, one could tell through simple observation that they were the closest of friends.

At last, the foursome rounded a corner and stood in front of an immense library with shiny marbled floors and high, arching columns at the end of each aisle. Rome had never seen one so huge. He put his hands on his hips and whistled.

The book aisles seemed to go on infinitely in both lateral directions. Comparatively, they seemed just as massive vertically as horizontally. There had to be thirty to forty shelves going upwards on each unit necessitating the use of sliding ladders to reach the highest levels. Rome peered down one of the lanes which continued for what seemed like forever until snaking off out of sight. There was no way of counting how many books this room held. Impressive was an understatement.

Julian punched Rome in the arm. "Mr. Jones would be in Heaven, huh Rome?" he said. "I can see him now blurting out something completely insane!" Rome agreed silently still awed by the sheer size of the collection. It would take an entire lifetime to read every book in this place. It made Rome's head hurt trying to comprehend how many hours of work he had in front of him. The task at hand was indeed daunting.

He stood dazed for a few seconds until he felt a tug on his sleeve. He looked over to see Krysta latched on with both of her arms. "C'mon, Rome," she said. "Let's head over to a table where we can discuss, converse, and get to know each other better." She led him to a table a few rows away from the entrance. The library was fairly busy, but they found a quiet spot where the group could have a powwow.

The four of them sat quietly for about a minute. Camela picked at her nails, and Julian rubbed his wrist. Much to Rome's surprise, Krysta rested her elbow on the table top with her chin inside her palm and gazed at him. Every now and then she would let out a sigh. It was not as uncomfortable as when Mrs. Case stared at him, but it was uncomfortable nonetheless.

Finally, Rome spoke up. "So, Camela. While we are here, your brother and I are doing a project on local legends. You know, oral tradition kind of stuff. We want to bring it back to The United States and do a comparative piece on folklore in America. We are hoping to get a lot of good material. I mean after all, this is where Camelot once stood, right?"

Camela looked up from her nails and narrowed her eyes. "What doest thou know of the gilded kingdom of Camelot, knave?" she squeaked.

"Well," stammered Rome. "I know that the good King Arthur set up his utopian society there. I know that his kingdom flourished under the watchful eye of his round table knights, and that his measures are sometimes considered the source roots of modern Democracy. Jules and I are more interested in all the mythological zoology that abounded the Camelot legends. We want to research folklore around the area pertaining to things less historical like dragons and such. We were hoping..."

Camela slammed her palms down on the table and stood up as tall as her five foot frame allowed her to. "Dragons," she shrieked. "You wish to fill your head and the heads of your classmates with such trivialities and nonsense as the possibility of dragons! I begin to wonder which person before me is the bigger fool. My brother refrains from opening his mouth about such gibberish so at least his audience knows not how big a fool he can be."

"Thanks?" shrugged Julian

Camela continued her tirade. "The same cannot be said for you, Rome of Canton. If you ever were to hear a tale of a dragon, it would undoubtedly be dishonesties spewed forth by the tongue of a criminal or drunkard soaked in libations. Furthermore, if anyone were to claim to have seen a dragon, they should be destined to suffer the horrific afterlife of prevaricators and perjurers. There are no such things as dragons, but if there were, it would be the first time our planet could actually benefit from the complete and total eradication of a species. Keep your infantile fantasies relegated to the schoolyard or sandbox. Laughable imprudence! 'Tis a fool's errand you both employ here today."

Rome was frozen. He glanced at his brother for some kind of guidance, but Julian blinked and spread his hands. What had just transpired? Julian had been right about his little sister. She was just like her father. She was as anti-dragon as she could be. She was a handful.

Chapter Four

Camela sat back down. From seemingly nowhere, she pulled out a book and began reading silently. Both Rome and Julian sat for about thirty seconds expecting her to say something more. Was she giving them the "silent treatment"? Finally, Krysta spoke up.

"Lady Camela," she urged. "Your brother and his friend just want to know about some ghost stories or local legends. I don't think they fully intend to write an expose' on dragons in the county of Somerset. It sounds rather harmless to me." She winked at Rome. "Perhaps we could just guide them to where they may find some information, statistics, or factoids here in our library."

Camela set her book down. "Very well, Krysta," she said. "You are as gifted an advisor as you are a protector." She looked at the boys. "I will assist you cantankerous clods, but only from my associates' insistence. Since your topic is that of a child's fancy, I would start in the children's literature section. It is over on the far left side by the mural of teddy bears frolicking in a forest of figmental flowers. There you will find tall tales and imaginative poppycock aplenty. Then, should you hunger for more delusion, I would try looking through old newspapers kept on digital file by the study stations."

"Sounds like a plan," said Julian rubbing his hands together. He looked at Rome. "What do you say we split up and try to find something intriguing for our project? I'll take the kid's lit section, and you give the newspapers a try."

"Yes," agreed Camela. "It would serve you both best to keep Julian's focus on par with that of his reading level." Once again, she buried her nose in her book.

"You've got it coming to you, ya little brat!" threatened Julian. "One day soon, I am gonna teach you a lesson that...." Krysta stood up from the table and crossed her arms. She glared at Julian. "But that's gonna have to wait for now because my wrist is still really sore, and I have those errands to run later......" He trailed off as he fled the table in search of the Children's Literature section.

Rome too pushed back his chair and stood up to exit the table. He noticed Krysta had uncrossed her arms and was smiling at him again. Her demeanor had softened significantly. Rome felt a little awkward when she came to his side of the table and grabbed his hand.

"I'll help you out, Rome" she said as a patch of her dancing hair tickled his neck. "Those machines can be quite frustrating, maddening, and impossible to use if you haven't operated them before. Besides, this will give us a little time alone. I want to help, assist, and support you and Sir Julian if I can." She spun her head around to face her friend. "Lady Camela, would it be okay if I escorted Rome to the periodical lexicons?"

Camela did not look up from her book, but she did make a dismissive gesture as she spoke. "If you wish to soil your honor by associating with those well below your status, I cannot hold you back, Krysta. However, we will need to be leaving shortly, so please keep a keen eye on the time."

Krysta squeezed Rome's hand tightly and did a little dance in place. Krysta let out a few audible giggles as she virtually dragged Rome to where the licensed computers sat. She flashed another smile at Rome when they reached their destination. She pulled out the chair for him, sat him in it, and turned him to face the most archaic piece of technological hardware he had ever seen.

The monitor was an old-school oscilloscope CRT about the size of a fish tank. It was bulky and had too many tangled wires popping out of it to count. Rome was sure he saw steam emitting from the thing as he powered up the decrepit CPU tower screwed into the table on his right. After he cleared the DOS screen, another mechanical device on the table began humming a disturbing drone. It was a rather obtuse, clunky machine with a monitor and what looked to be a scrolling device attached to where a keyboard would normally be stationed

"What is that thing?" asked Rome fearfully. "It sounds on the verge of exploding."

Krysta laughed out loud. Then, she swatted him playfully on the shoulder. "Rome, you are so funny. I assure you it is safe, secure, and perfectly harmless. It's called a microfiche viewer. It's a totally outdated gadget that people used to comb through old newspaper stories, documents, and articles. We may be able to find something useful, interesting, and pertinent to your project. Let me show you how to use it."

She moved in close to Rome, laying her hand on top of his. She guided it gently over to the scrolling device on the microfiche machine. Rome noticed the aromatic smell of fresh snow and pines emanating from Krysta. She turned her face towards his and sighed yet again.

"The articles are stored by year, month, and day accordingly," she said. "I'm not sure how far back they go, but we could start with the earliest on file then proceed, investigate, and discover anything relevant. To help us out, I can cross reference certain words in the articles if you would like."

Rome nodded in approval. He was impressed with how she maneuvered the device so delicately and yet with such accuracy and speed. Couple her precise, fluid movements with her apparent martial arts knowledge, and she could be quite a contributive ally. No wonder Camela had enlisted her as a personal watchdog. "So, where do you want to start, Rome?" she giggled.

"Well," he shrugged. "I am not sure. What do you suggest?"

Krysta clapped her hands together three times and smiled at him. "I think we should search for prominent words you want to find in the articles. It will automatically put them in order from oldest to most recent. Although it's pretty outdated, the program we have can act like a search engine like Google, Yahoo, or Lycos. I would suggest searching for the words 'dragon', 'monster', and... 'handsome'.

Rome looked at her sideways. "Maybe just try 'dragon' and 'monster'. He turned back to face the screen.

"Yeah, you're right," Krysta agreed. "We don't need to search for 'handsome'. I've already found it." Rome blushed slightly.

Together, the two began perusing the articles that the program pulled up. At first, they checked only the headlines hoping to find something about an encounter or an eye witness testimony. Rome found multitudes of incidents involving spectators seeing bright lights in the sky over the southern hills and incredible tales of people coming face to face with the unexplained. Most of the stories seemed like hoaxes to Rome. He read about a woman who claimed to see an elongated worm-like creature in the local lake which swam through the water like an eel. He read about a local homeless man who claimed to have been bitten by an extremely hairy human standing over eight feet tall. He found droves of conflicting tales of demons and poltergeists and half-human hybrid sightings resulting in savage confrontation.

He felt like he was about to succumb to jet lag when he finally came across a specific article that made his usually fiery blood turn ice cold. It was about a man who was camping in the woods near the local lake when he encountered what he described as "a hideous wolf-like creature tromping by the beach". He claimed that the creature approached his campfire during the early, evening hours. He described a monstrous wolf that "roared screeches sounding like pure evil, Gov!" He claimed the monster charged him and violently destroyed his campsite as if driven by madness. The man deserted the site, jumped in his truck one hundred yards away, and drove home as fast as he could. He told authorities that he would never go back into those woods until someone killed the beast. Apparently, local law enforcement scavenged the woods for an entire day, but never turned up anything except the man's destroyed campsite. The article was dated from the winter of the previous year.

"Eureka!" shouted Rome. "I think we have

a starting point. I can probably track down this guy and get him to tell me his whole story. His story sounds both relevant and unusual."

Krysta lit up. "Oh, Rome, that's great," she said. "I knew you would find something helpful. Maybe we can celebrate this occasion with dinner, a movie, and some snuggling."

"Uh, that is okay, Krysta," Rome stammered. "I really want to get with Julian and follow up on this lead. I will take a raincheck? Is that cool?"

"Um hmmmmm," she responded positively. "You had better get going while it's fresh in your head. I'm so proud of, happy for, and excited for you. I know I am assigned to Lady Camela, but I want you to know that I will be willing to help, assist, and direct you if need be." She started to walk back towards Camela who was standing near the exit tapping her pintsized foot emphatically. Krysta looked back at Rome and gave him a wink. "I'll be watching over you, Rome. Just in CASE you need my protection as well."

As she walked away, Rome took notice of Krysta's cursive hair again. It seemed to continually prance in an invisible wind. The golden locks swirled like independent tendrils all the way down to the snow-white tips. Rome sensed an almost magical essence creating the hypnotic movements that seemed to defy gravity.

Rome briefly considered talking to Julian about enlisting Krysta as a personal bodyguard for them in case they found themselves in a sticky situation overseas. She was skillful and intelligent and somewhat fascinating. Somewhere in his mind he heard a resounding "NO" on the spatial linking from his brother. There went Julian reading Rome's thoughts again. Rome immediately understood that having Krysta around meant having Camela around. They both agreed that could be the worst decision they made during their stay in England. Rome realized that Julian was right when he described his younger sister. She was fervently set in her ideas of dragons most likely thanks to her upbringing. She was commanding and strong-willed and most definitely conniving. She certainly was a handful.

Chapter Five

Julian sent another spatial link message to Rome telling him to come see him in the Children's Literature section. Rome waved goodbye to the girls who were apparently "well beyond our departure time". He then headed to where Camela had originally directed her older brother. Rome wondered if Julian had found something bigger than what he had discovered, but he doubted that was the case. He envisioned Julian making a huge fuss about a collection of fairy tales or some touch and feel book with dragon scales. Among other individualistic personality traits, Julian was highly prone to hyperbole.

As Rome walked by the many aisles of the library he was once again overcome by the absolute enormity of the place. There were literally endless rows of books hibernating on the monstrous shelves. There was so much paper in this room that Rome would certainly have to be careful with his eye auras. It would only take one stray flicker to turn the whole place into a towering inferno.

From where Rome was, he could see the enormous flower decals on the wall. They were certainly a long way off, but it did not matter to Rome. He thoroughly enjoyed his voyage through the library and some time to himself to contemplate the next steps. He knew his lead was a perfect starting point for them to follow. There was already a plethora of burning questions floating around in Rome's cerebellum he wanted to ask the man who had survived a Garm attack. Also, he wanted to advise him to go play the lottery for being so lucky to survive the encounter.

Rome approached Julian who was sitting on a chair that was ludicrously too small for him. He had his feet resting on one of his conjured frying pans, and he was flipping through the pages of a comic book. He saw Rome coming, so he stood up and tossed the comic book to him.

"Check it out, dude," said Julian as he juggled his die back and forth in the air. "I found that at the bottom of a huge pile. They've got a pretty good collection here for a bunch of dorks." Rome found it uproarious that Julian concentrated his search in the comic book section. What was next? A sweeping investigation of the school's

Manga selections?

Rome flipped the book to its cover. It read "Knights of Camelot". The front cover showed a picture of a knight in full regalia riding on top of a fire breathing dragon. The dragon was wrestling with what appeared to be a large monster with the head of a bull. Underneath the title, it read "Lancelot meets his biggest challenge yet. The Minotaur!" It was quite compelling evidence. Rome was impressed with Julian's find. Like Mr. Jones had originally told them, the portion of history that was lost to legend could be found all around them. You just needed to know what you were looking for. This work of fiction was a clear depiction of a Synergist Knight and Dragon Master taking on one of the foul Darkbrand army.

"So, according to this, Lancelot was a Synergist Knight," said Rome. "I thought only the House of Rider was able to perform The Great Synergy?"

"Well," started Julian. "I think this is an embellishment. I mean no one knows who my great, great, great, great, great, great, great, great grandfather was, but EVERYONE has heard of Sir Lancelot. That's probably how the details got mucked as it was passed down through the generations. Also, dude, you have to remember that there were other knights completing the ritual during the second wave of the Darkbrand invasion. Earth's forces were doing everything they could to create an army strong enough to repel The Tyrant King's minions. All walks of warriors and dragons were joining the resistance and pledging their lives to The Great Synergy. My family just happened to be the first and last bloodline to carry this out. We are the only ones left."

"So, in theory," Rome expounded. "Camela could be a Synergist Knight if she found a dragon to bond with? Would she join our resistance?"

"Well, yeah," stammered Julian. "But you've seen how she is. She's just like my dad. She's a total dragon hater. She would never join the fight if it involved The Great Synergy. I'm pretty sure she is the furthest thing from an ally we have at this point." Julian stuffed his die in his pocket. "And besides, where would we find another dragon on such short notice? You think your parents want to join our cause?"

Julian was right, but Rome was intrigued by the idea that Julian's relatives could be Synergist Knights. His capricious companion had also forgot to mention that they were still not exactly sure how to execute The Great Synergy anyway. As far as they knew, the die had been the cardinal key to unlocking their powers and forcing a shared heart, but Mr. Jones was still not convinced it was performed as originally intended. He thought something was still missing. Almost as if they had only scratched the surface of The Great Synergy's potential.

Rome studied the cover of the comic book for a second then started back down his opening thought stream. "What about any other family? Do you have any cousins with a knack for procuring kitchen ware out of thin air?"

Julian snickered. "Very funny, dude. My father was an only child so I have no blood cousins who could take up arms with us. I mean, theoretically there could be members from other families that are alive today, but I seriously doubt it. Mr. Jones said he believes all the other bloodlines were severed as far back as he can research. That's why I'm so special!"

"Oh, you are special, alright," quipped Rome. "We need to keep this comic book for research, but I want to show you what I found in the old newspaper articles. I think I have found a really hot lead."

"Fire dragon hot?" asked Julian.

Rome put out his knuckles for Julian to fist bump. "You know it, Jules."

After a few minutes of Julian pleading with Rome to let him stay and read some more comics, the boys meandered back to where the microfiche machine was still humming along. Julian sarcastically pointed out that the machine appeared ready to explode. He even poked it a couple times with the handle of the frying pan he had conjured as a footrest back in the children's section.

Begrudgingly, they sat down, and Julian began reading the article. As he was perusing the print, Rome's dragon ears perked up. He was getting a funny feeling they were being watched. He calmly scanned the library for anything unusual. Then, he saw it. The humanoid shadow figure that had stalked him back home. It was darting behind a large file cabinet near the fire escape and peeking out from behind it. Rome saw the glowing red orb which lit up the surrounding piles of books. What was she doing HERE???? Had she followed him?

Rome felt the burn in his eyes starting up. If the figure wanted to finally step out of the shadows and face off against the boys, Rome would gladly comply. Quickly, he realized that they could not afford a confrontation here with all the witnesses and flammable material. Mr. Jones had instilled in them the rule to remain undercover while they toured England. Discretion was after all the better part of valor. Rome watched impotently as the figure disappeared out of sight into the shadows of the library corridors. He clenched his fist and vowed to uncover the truth behind that menace. She was so smart to follow him into a public place bounded by so much combustible tinder that he could not exert his powers.

"This is amazing!" shouted Julian breaking Rome's concentration. One boy at another table gave Julian an angry hush before getting back to his studies. "Dude, do you realize what you've found?" Julian was hardly able to contain his emotions. "This is a documented encounter with a Garm, bro!" Again, the boy shushed Julian. "We gotta talk to this guy and see what he can tell us. It says here that he's a local."

"Yeah," agreed Rome changing gears. "But how can we get his personal information?"

Julian was still basically screaming. "Dude, we have our own personal wizard back home that can probably find him with one of his crazy spells. He's like an old-school internet database that lives in a library. We just need to call him tonight. Or send him a telegram. I don't know how old people communicate, man."

The boy at the nearby table slammed his book closed, gave Julian a menacing look, and walked to another part of the library. Julian watched him leave then looked to Rome with a "what did I do" face.

Rome agreed that Julian's idea was worth a try. Although Mr. Jones wasn't really a wizard by any means, he was quite resourceful. His knowledge of the histories and reemergence novella were barely overshadowed by his cunning and spell mastery. He had already amazed the boys on a few occasions with some well-placed tricks up his sleeve. Maybe he moonlighted as a human phone book too.

Rome stood back to watch his blood brother rereading the article with wide eyes and whispering lips. They were a really good team. They had only been in town for a day, and they had already found two unlikely, but helpful associates and pinpointed a great lead while digging up some literature to support Mr. Jones's theories. He would be very proud of his young warriors. They were steadily putting their plan into action of eliminating portals. If they could uncover details to help them foil The Tyrant King's vicious agenda, then putting up with Camela could be considered a minor issue. The world was going to need their powers, and the boys were ready to do battle like the knights and dragons of old. Little did they know, their toughest challenges were waiting for them in the countryside of Somerset, and it would take all their guile and strength to overcome them.

Chapter Six

The boys, being completely innocent to the evil percolating in the nearby woods, decided to take their time getting back to their dorm room. They walked along the streets of the quaint town and took in all the sights they could. They followed a local river under one of the bridges in town and skipped rocks from above. They took some pictures by a few statues modeled after classic characters from Arthurian legends. They even stopped at a local eatery to give the English flavor a crack.

"I am starving. What do you want off the menu today?" inquired Rome.

"Well," said Julian. "I guess we should try something local. You know what they say? When in Rome..."

"Your humor does not miss a beat, does it Jules?" Rome groaned.

Without a second's hesitation, Julian

decided. "Let's try the fish and chips, Gov'ner."

Both of the boys agreed that it was an "acquired taste". Of course they both devoured the chips portion of the meal with little hesitance. The fish, on the other hand was mostly pushed around and left in their baskets. Rome liked it okay, but steered clear of the accompanying mushy peas. Julian wouldn't touch his fish, but guzzled down ramekin after ramekin of malt vinegar while Rome looked on horrified. What a pair they were!

Rome was very thankful that Julian's father had financed the entire trip for the boys. He still wasn't sure what Mr. Rider did for a living, but he was sure it must be pretty lucrative. Julian told Rome they would not want for anything for the duration of this expedition. Rome was humbled by the man's generosity even though Mr. Rider was a total weirdo. I mean, who wears capes?

The boys joked and laughed the whole way back to the dorms. It was amazing how quickly they had become best friends. Perhaps it was a side effect of The Great Synergy, but the boys clearly got along well. Although their personalities and interests were on opposite ends of the spectrum, they just clicked as brothers. It was not as if they didn't have differences that clashed on multiple occasions. It was just that below all those differences there was a deep-running respect for each other as both fighters and partners. They knew they would have each other's backs for the rest of their lives. No ancient ritual could fake that.

Luckily, the dorm room contained a phone that allowed the boys to make calls back to The United States at all hours of the day. They could easily dial home virtually whenever they wanted to. Mr. Rider had provided them with room and board as well as unlimited funds for long distance calls by setting up a call account

"Let's call Mr. Jones at the library," suggested Julian.

"Jules," argued Rome. "The hour is late afternoon here. That means it is super early back home. Do you think Mr. Jones will be just hanging around the library?"

"Well, yeah," huffed Julian. "I think he lives there, man."

"Okay," submitted Rome. "Give him a call"

Julian picked up the portable handset and jumped on his bed. Rome was a little surprised because he had only seen a few landline phones in his life. It was a sign of the times that fewer people were using anything other than cellular these days. Everyone Rome knew had a cell phone and a family plan. The idea of the family phone and all the sharing hassles that came with it was all but extinct. That was kind of the way Rome felt sometimes. He struggled with thoughts about being alone in the world. He was never really alone, because he had his blood brother and Mr. Jones, but as far as he knew, he was the only dragon left. Maybe he was the last one of his race. He was kind of like the landline phone service of Earth's species.

It wasn't long before Julian was pushing a bunch of buttons and typing in passcodes to get his long distance account on line. The boys would probably need to call home every other day or so with reports for Mr. Jones and to check in with their parents. Rome knew he would miss his parents soon enough. Right now, though, he was really excited to be sniffing out clues and hunting for Darkbrands.

Again, Rome's conflicting thoughts rattled around his brain. He loved his parents, but he wanted to know why they had never told him about his heritage. Mr. Jones said they probably did not even know themselves that they were dragons. Rome figured one day he would need to tell them. Or maybe, it was better that they stay in the dark about this so they would not worry about being persecuted by the likes of Mr. Rider and others. Maybe to protect them, he should never tell them.

"It's ringing!" shouted Julian while doing his patented ninja jump kick off the bed. He placed the phone on the nightstand in between the boys' beds and pressed the speakerphone button. Both boys huddled around the phone in great anticipation. The phone rang a couple more times when finally a very out of breath Mr. Jones picked up the call.

"Hello....boys!" he gasped. "Are you there? You nearly gave me a heart attack. No one ever calls this number anymore. By the horns of Taurus! It most definitely took me by surprise! I think the last time the library phone rang, the Atlanta Braves were in the World Series."

Rome had missed his teacher's ramblings. It was good to hear his voice. Mr. Jones was not only the information wellspring of this team, but also the strategist. Both boys knew this overseas mission would be tough without their advisor, but they were willing to take on the challenge for the sake of their planet.

"Hey, old man," said Julian. "It's good to hear your voice." Julian must have been picking up on Rome's thoughts again. "But you gotta slow your roll and chill out for a minute. We have a lot to update you on. How can we let you know all we've learned if you keep jabbering on and on?" There was the old Julian!

"Great griffin's plumes!" retorted Mr. Jones. "My apologies gentlemen. I also meant to say that we have no need for trivialities such as a telephone. We can make use of much more sorcerous endeavors. See you in a jiffy!"

"What are you talking about, old man?" erupted Julian. He glanced at Rome for assistance, but Rome spread his hands weakly. "Hey, Mr. Jones...Mr. Jones! Old man!!!!!"

"Did he hang up?" wondered Rome.

"The line is dead, dude," said Julian. He slammed the phone down on the receiver. "Crazy old coot! I was really looking forward to telling him about my comic book!"

"And what comic book would that be?" came a

familiar voice from inside the room.

Julian literally jumped into Rome's arms. "Ahhhhhhhhhh!" screamed Julian.

Standing before the two boys, chewing on his glasses, was Mr. Jones. He smiled coyly as he crossed his arms. "Ta-da," he said.

Julian started in on the elderly librarian. "What the heck, dude!!?? You trying to kill me or something? What are you doing here? Did you come through the phone line?"

Mr. Jones moved to a chair occupying the corner of the dorm room and sat down. "Transportation Incantation," he said with a bit of a laugh. Mr. Jones bounced in the recliner and looked around the room. "Of all the Hydra's heads, this is a very nice setup you have here. And this is a really comfortable chair!"

"Yes," strained Julian. "My father had it shipped here from London especially for me and Rome to relax in while we are brainstorming ideas on how to save the world. So, now that we know why the CHAIR is here, maybe you can tell us what YOU are doing here!"

"Of course," chuckled Mr. Jones. "I wanted to

see you guys and bring you good news. I have made several stops by your school to verify that the portal has been permanently sealed. Multiple times, I have viewed it through my magic glasses and determined that it is no longer a threat to us. Marvelous job boys!" He hesitated before staring at them sideways. "I also brought a memento for you fellas to have during your time over here."

Mr. Jones reached into his pocket and pulled out the tip of the horn the boys found during their last battle at Dampier Middle School. He held it close to his face at first as if admiring the abnormality. Then, he retracted as if it had seriously offended his sense of smell.

"Thanks to you, this is all that breached the gap of our two worlds. I am quite sure that somewhere in that impenetrable darkness, there is one very angry Minotaur missing the tip of its stately horn. I have been unable to locate it in The Void, but I am sure it is quite peeved, as one may say." Mr. Jones tossed the fragment to Julian who caught it in an exaggerated way. He held it out for Rome to see.

"Let's hope we never run into what was once connected to this, bro," said Julian.

Mr. Jones spoke again. "I am very proud of you boys. Yet, I am also very interested. What, if any discoveries have you already made here in England? I must also warn you that my connection here is not indefinite. I will only be able to sustain this conference for an hour or so."

Rome and Julian brought Mr. Jones up to speed as fast as they could. They told him about the article they found in the library, the girls, and Julian boasted proudly about his comic book discovery. They discussed possible avenues for investigation in order to find out if there was a portal in the vicinity. Mr. Jones agreed with the boys that they needed to interview the man from the newspaper article as soon as possible. There was a chance that his testimony may even lead them to the location of a portal. Julian suggested they attend a comic book convention, but was abruptly shot down by both Rome and Mr. Jones.

"So, how do we find this guy?" asked Rome. "I mean, this is a small town, but it would take us forever to find him. All we have is a first and last name."

"Young Master," soothed Mr. Jones. "You also have a magician. I will use my Transportation Incantation to "jump" you boys to his exact location. It will be quite flawless much like how I used to teleport you boys inside the school without you even noticing." Mr. Jones smiled to himself.

Rome's dragon eyes were getting very tired, but he wanted to mention the shadow figure he saw in the library to Mr. Jones as well. Before he could mention it, Julian pounced on him and punched him in the arm.

"Dude, why didn't you tell me you saw that creepy lady again? We could have blasted her! I'm not always tuned into your head, dude. Sometimes you have to share with me. I can't read your mind all the time. Truth be told, it's kind of a strange place in there."

"Probably because it is reptilian," teased Rome. "Sorry, Jules. I should have mentioned it for sure."

Mr. Jones frowned and rubbed his chin. "So, that means the shadowy figure has followed you from America. This is of definite concern, boys. As I have told you many times, there are other pieces on this figurative chessboard, but I am left in the dark as to their intentions. I suggest we only confront the shadow figure if provoked. I know it may be hard to imagine because of its eerie penchant for the stalking you, but this person may actually be an ally observing from afar. Let us leave her alone for now. She will come into the light at the appropriate time."

Mr. Jones glanced at the clock on the wall. "For now, I suggest you boys get some sleep. I will arrive tomorrow after your classes and transport you to the gentleman's location. I want to once again tell you how proud I am of you two. If there is indeed a portal in this town, I am sure you will find it and dispose of it. Goodnight, gentlemen."

Mr. Jones faded from the room like Star Trek characters being beamed back onboard the Starship Enterprise. Julian tossed the Minotaur horn in his left hand and tossed his magic die in his right. The boys sat in silence for a few moments before Julian spoke up.

"You heard the old geezer, Rome. Time to get some sleep. We've got a long day of searching for a shadow person and questioning some dude about his encounter with a monster from The Void. It's gonna be so awesome!"

Well, Rome should have known that Julian would be overly excited about the chance to hunt a Garm. Maybe it was the nature of humans to be constantly testing and pushing themselves further. Julian almost reveled in the thought of battle. Rome could feel how eager Julian got both times they had confronted the bloodthirsty creatures. Rome had been nervous and worried he would screw something up. How different dragons and humans looked at the world. It was as if the two species were never meant to coexist on this planet. Then why was there The Great Synergy? It was the ritual that completed the dragon heart and created the eternal bond between knight and dragon. It was like nothing else in the universe. No! Rome knew there was a reason for The Great Synergy. There was a destiny behind his meeting Julian and beginning their crusade against the Darkbrands. Even if the boys had performed The Great Synergy out of necessity, Rome knew how strong they were as one. Rome knew the potential and power they had. As long as they worked together, there was nothing they couldn't handle, right?

Chapter Seven

The next morning, the boys were up early. They were even ready before everyone else on their hall. The rules of the dormitory were pretty simple. All students were to get dressed and be standing outside their rooms by 8:15. At that point, the chaperones did a head count, and they all walked to the educational portion of the building in two separate lines; boys on the right and girls on the left. Though it seemed pretty sophomoric, Rome could understand the need for such stringent structure. Here they were, overseas, and the last thing the school needed was to lose a student. Or a chaperone.

As the boys went to the classroom where they would be receiving their international education, Rome realized he had not even been to a single class yet. They had only been there for less than a day, but Rome had not learned anything scholastic at all. He had been so distracted with finding evidence of portal activity that he had forgotten the original reason for their sabbatical.

Riders of Fire and Ice

The classroom where they studied was nothing short of remarkable. The seats were stadium-style forming a half circle around the chamber and extended about twelve rows upwards. Each seat was granted so much elbow room that every student virtually had his own office space. Every desk had things like docks for laptops and electrical outlets for charging student's learning devices. The half circle formed columns around the room with the teacher standing and orating in the center of the pit. It was much different from the tiny, drab-brown desks the boys were used to stateside.

Rome sat quietly in his chair and tried to pay attention to the many professors who conducted lessons that day. He noticed their different accents and their much different ways of instruction. They were very high energy and intriguing to listen to. Rome thought if he could understand them better, this would be a much more beneficial way of learning. No wonder these kinds of schools charged admission, room, and board. Rome decided that if he ever attended a university or school that required tuition, he would make sure to get the most out of it.

Halfway through the day, the students

broke for lunch. This gave the American pupils a chance to visit the common area where the boarding school students spent their free time. Both the girl's finishing school for ladies and the boy's preparatory institute used the common area for extracurricular activities. It was the only chance all three assemblages would get to interact with each other during the school day. Rome was kind of relieved when he finally got to the common area.

He walked timidly into the expanse where at least fifty students meandered around socializing and playing games. Rome even saw a small group of students playing hackey sack again. He motioned to Julian to head that way. Rome hoped to find solace and relatability in the circle of students enjoying Rome's favorite hobby.

He started to head over to the group, when he felt a cool hand on his shoulder. He stopped in his tracks half expecting it to be Mrs. Case coming to creep him out some more. As he slowly turned his head, he was pleasantly surprised to see Krysta Valanche standing behind him eating a Popsicle.

"Hey there, Rome," she said smiling wide. "Are you enjoying your lunch break? I thought I would come by and see if there was anything you needed, wanted, or expected."

"Oh, Krysta," sighed Rome. "It does me good to see you. I think I am doing just fine. I was going to go see if I could get in that hackey sack circle. Do you want to join?"

From somewhere behind Krysta came a shrill voice that sounded like nails running down a chalkboard. "Silly knave. We haven't time for such frivolities as you commoners. To what purpose does one hope to accomplish repeatedly bouncing a clothed bean bag into the air anyway? Methinks 'tis more of a waste of time than observing paint drying on a wall."

Camela poked her head out from behind Krysta. Then she moved to stand directly beside her bodyguard. She blew a pink bubble from the gum she was chewing which popped loudly. "Perhaps it is the ones with the least amount of brain cells that derive the most pleasure from kicking a sack."

"It's fun!" interjected Julian. "When was the last time you had any fun, you little terror? Lemme guess. It was when dad bought you that Joan of Arc bookcase, and you spent the whole day organizing your library numerically by which century they were written in."

Camela popped another bubble. "That WAS a magical day of my youth." She paused as if relishing the memory. "Wasn't that the same day you trapped your fat head in the refrigerator crisper?"

"Camela!" yelled Julian. He leapt at her with his hands in a strangling position. But before he could get within a foot of her, Krysta drove her knee into his stomach, spun around on the ground, and leg swept him to the floor. He fell hard, and the back of his head made a vicious impact with the linoleum.

Immediately Krysta was helping him to his feet. "I'm truly sorry," she said. "But I've already told you that I can't have anyone threatening, challenging, or strangling Lady Camela." She reached into her lunchbox and pulled out an ice pack. "Hold this to the back of your head. It will feel better soon." She regarded Rome for a second. "Are you okay Rome? Do you need some ice too?"

Rome looked at her curiously. What did she mean? He hadn't fallen down. She hadn't injured HIM. He was merely a witness to Krysta's ever increasing mastery of the Martial Arts. Then, he felt the throb in the back of his head. Once again, The Great Synergy made Rome feel Julian's aches. He clenched his teeth and squinted his eyes. The pain was mild, but it was a headache nonetheless.

"No, I'm okay," he managed. He scratched his head to make it seem like he was confused by her offering. How did she know he would feel Julian's pain? Maybe she was just asking if he wanted some ice. Maybe.

"Well, as usual, we must be off before we can truly be exposed to the folly of my elder sibling," chortled Camela. "Perhaps our next visit will involve more intelligent banter and less falling on one's hindquarters. We are late for equestrian class. Goodbye"

She turned and started moving towards the exit of the student center. Her little legs shuffled across the floor making her look like a pig-tailed penguin. Krysta turned to follow her, but stopped for a second to speak to the boys.

"Rome," she said. "It was a pleasure, a joy, and a delight seeing you again. See you around!" She giggled and turned to catch up to her friend. What a strange relationship those two had. They were like a morbid version of good cop/bad cop.

Julian rubbed his head and stared at the duo walking away. "One of these days," he warned angrily. "C'mon, Rome. Let's go see about getting in that hackey sack circle."

"Real quick, Jules," said Rome. "Did you hear what Krysta said to me?"

"Naw, dude," he retorted. "I couldn't hear anything over the ringing in my ears. That girl is mean!"

Rome laughed to himself. It really wasn't a big deal. There was no way she could know the boys' secret anyway. They had just met yesterday! Unless she was somehow connected to the shadow figure stalking him. Maybe she WAS the shadow figure? Rome quickly put that thought out of his mind. Krysta was just an average girl who had some of Camela's strangeness rub off on her from hanging out with her for so long. The idea that Camela was like some kind of weird virus that spread to people she spent time with made Rome laugh again. He hoped he did not contract whatever Camela was contaminating the world with.

"That's right bro," said Julian. "She IS like some kind of nutcase bacteria or something."

Both boys laughed out loud.

They spent the rest of their break in the hackey-sack circle getting to know some of the kids from the private institutions. When break time was over, they went back to their classroom to finish the day. Julian and Rome were really excited to be done with classes so they could resume their plan to interview the man who had seen the Garm in the woods by the lake.

When they finally got back to their dorm for the evening, the boys gathered their things and prepared for the events to come. Julian grabbed the Minotaur horn and put it in his pocket. Rome packed a small book bag with pens and paper in case they needed to write down directions or any special notes. He also put the comic book in the bag in case Julian got bored with the conversation. Rome did not even need to read his brother's thoughts to know that Julian would probably lose interest at some point during their meeting.

"Good looking out," said Julian as they awaited contact from Mr. Jones. "I should probably bring my iPad so I can play Candy Crush too."

As the boys sat in great anticipation, Mr. Jones materialized in the middle of their room. However, he wasn't fully there. He was blinking in and out like an old television with fuzzy reception. Through the static interference, the boys were able to make out his words through concentration.

"The Transportation Incantation only has so much strength, so I have to focus most of my attention on you boys." He disappeared and reappeared in quick bursts which made it very hard to follow even with Rome's dragon eyes. "I need you boys to focus on the man's name so I can locate him in space and time. It would help if you said his name out loud too."

The boys looked at each other and then back at the flickering Mr. Jones. "Titus S. Thompson," they said aloud simultaneously.

"Very good boys," Mr. Jones said before he vanished out of sight. A few seconds passed and the boys began to look around the room. Maybe the incantation had failed. Nothing seemed to be happening.

Instantaneously, they were standing before

a dark house on the outskirts of a short driveway. The house itself seemed rather ordinary. It was a one-story, ranch-style home with a brick exterior. There was a small porch which extended from the front door to the left about ten feet. There sat a lonely rocking chair with fading and chipping white paint. The house appeared to be in need of some upkeep, but its rustic look reflected the quaintness of it over all. Although they were in a neighborhood, there was overgrowth of flora on all sides of the house. In fact, the backyard looked completely overrun with wild shrubbery and trees that seemed to come from the Mesozoic Era.

The boys looked at each other again. Rome exhaled sharply, and Julian laughed nervously. Just like before when they had entered the school with the incantation, they both reached their destination safely and in one piece Back then, they had not even observed the enchantment as their origin and end points were basically the same. However, this time the jump was much more noticeable since they had switched locations. Being surrounded by the confines of a disheveled dormitory and then suddenly appearing outside a home in the evening English air was quite jarring to the senses. Also, space/time was a concept beyond the boys' comprehension for now.

Rome turned to face Julian. "Time???!!" he said out loud. "We do not have a lot of time, Jules."

"You can say that again," exclaimed Julian. He slowly began to raise his hands in the air.

Rome turned back to the house to see a shaky, shoeless man standing on the front porch with a very intimidating shotgun pointed right at the boys. This was not a good start.

Chapter Eight

Rome and Julian were frozen in fear. They stood like two rigid statues sculpted directly into the asphalt at their feet. Neither one flinched or breathed for what seemed like forever. Rome's brain came online first. He sent a frantic message to Julian using their spatial linking ability.

"Should we run, Jules?" asked Rome with grave concern

"No way, man. We have got to talk to this guy."

"How do we even know this is the right guy?"

"I trust the old fellow and his magic. He has never led us astray before."

"Should we transform and bombard him?"

"That might be the best idea you've ever had," replied Julian

81

Before Julian could make a move to get his shaky hands on his magical die, the man shouted to them.

"Oi, lads!" he said in a very thick, British accent. "Better get on home to your mums 'for it gets dark. There be an evil in the woods beyond the lake. Ya would not catch me ahhht after dark, and you can bet your brass on that."

Julian spoke up. "Are you Mr. Thompson? Mr. Titus S. Thompson?"

The man lowered his gun muzzle to the ground. "Aye," he sneered. "An' who wants to know it?"

Julian lowered his hands and spoke with more gumption. "Sir, my name is Julian and this is my friend Rome. We were hoping to talk to you about an incident that took place in those woods a few months ago. Would you mind answering a few questions for us?"

Mr. Thompson placed his gun down near the doorway. He walked in tiny circles five or six times, then sat down in the rocking chair. He eyed the boys while he took a pipe from his pocket and stuck it to his lips. He did not light it.

"Americans, huh? Yer not from the tabloids, are ya?" he asked.

This time Rome spoke up. "No, sir," he said. "We are doing a school project on local folklore and the supernatural. We read in an article that you may have had an encounter with something extraordinary. May we approach you, sir?"

Mr. Thompson hopped up from his chair, did a few jumping jacks, and then sat back down and glared at the boys. "Aye," he said. "And ya best hurry yer arses. You'd be daft to be stuck ahht here after dark." He knocked the pipe against the arm rail of his rocking chair, but nothing came out.

The boys looked at each other with astonished eyes. Julian let out a chuckle and started for the front door. Rome sent one more message to Julian warning him to be alert at all times. Mr. Thompson obviously had a couple screws loose. Not to mention the shotgun he had left at the side of the front door. There could be more guns elsewhere in the house.

Rome jogged to catch up with Julian, and the boys entered the house through the front door. Rome took one more look at the gun propped up against the door frame and inhaled sharply. He was really hoping he would not have to test out his dragon scales against the scatter shot of a Remington.

Once they entered the humble abode, Rome immediately wished he hadn't. From the entrance, Rome could see an absolute mess in the adjacent living room. There were piles of old clothes and magazines swarming with flies. The stench was equally as abysmal. It smelled like long forgotten milk and decaying fruit. Rome surmised that these were probably the reason the hoard of flies had taken up residence.

Mr. Thompson was pacing in the kitchen which was a few feet down the hallway from their entry point. He wore baggy, blue jean overalls but only one strap was securely fastened to its corresponding button. Beneath them was a plain, white undershirt with a few holes in the left shoulder. Rome once again noticed that he was without foot apparel as he pulled on his lip and muttered to himself vacantly. The boys walked towards him cautiously until he stopped abruptly and stared at the floor.

"C'mon in fellas," he mumbled. His eyes never left the floor, and they appeared to grow bigger as the boys approached. "What do you blokes wanna know?"

Julian treaded into the crazy waters first. "Uh, Mr. Thompson. The article said you ran into something out in the woods that could only be described as otherworldly. You said it attacked you. Can you give us a detailed description of whatever you saw?"

Mr. Thompson did not hesitate. In fact, he became quite erratic and verbally boisterous. "I can do you one better! I'll draw it fer ya!" He pulled a pencil from his sock and a blank sheet of notebook paper from his kitchen counter. He began to scribble feverishly on the paper and lick his lips.

Mr. Thompson ranted on as he drew. "Them woods are dodgy, mates! I grew up in this area, and I used to go fishing and boating on that lake with me dad every summer. I never seen anyfin' like that before. I believe I came face to face with pure evil. It was a werewolf. No, it was a lizard tiger. No, it was a wolf demon. But not like any wolf me peepers ever seen. The pelt was black as midnight with purple streaks up n'it." He paused to scratch his head emphatically as if he was scraping at fleas. "It had claws that could half a tree trunk. And teeth. Oi, the teeth were like buzz saws chomping for me knickers."

He slammed his pencil hard on the counter and handed over the drawing. Rome took it and held it out for both boys to view. Mr. Thompson had drawn two stick figures with over exaggerated smiles playing tennis. The ball in play looked more like a bowling ball, and it was on fire. Julian grinned finding some humor in the scene.

"Brothers, I tell you straight as me mum. There were tentacles on this thing's mug. All waving around like buggers." He put his hands to his face and violently wiggled his fingers, then made an animal-like sound which made the boys jump. "I know that beastie will haunt me dreams and Bob's your uncle."

As if his performance was over, he sat down on the floor Indian style and cradled his head in his hands. He whispered like he was telling someone who was not there. "It's got me gutted. Real fancy like."

Julian and Rome stood silently for a few minutes expecting another eruption. When Mr. Thompson began stroking his knee cap and blinking sporadically, the boys moved closer to each other. Using their spatial linking, they began a quick assessment of the situation.

"I believe this bloke is legit," said Julian.

"That's a pretty accurate description of a Garm. Should we press him for a location?" wondered Rome.

"How about another work of art?" joked Julian.

"I feel like we need to get out of here as soon as possible," remarked Rome.

"Okay, follow my lead, bro," decided Julian.

Julian Spoke to Mr. Thompson almost like an adult would talk to a child. "Okay, Mr. T. Thank you sooooo much for telling us about that scary monster. Would you be able to tell us where you found it? Or rather where it found you?"

To Rome's surprise, Mr. Thompson stood up quickly, grabbed a shoe from the kitchen counter, and launched it across the room into a corner. The boys followed the trajectory of the shoe and saw a handful of cockroaches scurrying away from where the shoe impacted the wall. Paranoia had most definitely intruded into Mr. Thompson's head and set up permanent residence.

"Aye, mates," said Mr. Thompson as he stared across the room at his shoe. "It's up by the lake. That's where I was making me camp that night. Head straight through the woods from my backyard for about three kilometers. You'll see a rock wall, you will. Turn right at the rock wall and go another kilometer. You'll come to that cursed lake. You should be able to see what's left of me camp down by the water's edge. A've not been back since that night."

He turned to look at the boys. "Ya sure yer not from the tabloids? I'd hate to send anybody to a certain death that's not affiliated with those mucker 'zines, ya know?" He picked up his other shoe and began talking into it like a telephone. "I can't talk to ya now, mum. A've got guests. I'll ring you tomorrow and we can go shopping for jellybeans. I don't know! Okay, I'll ask 'em." He covered the heel of the shoe as if he didn't want to let any background noise into the "receiver". "Me mum asked if you boys wanna come along. She usually pays for lunch and a pint. 'Course you lads probably won't be partakin' in the pint."

"No thank you, Mr. Thompson," said Julian back pedaling. "It sounds like you and your "mum" should spend the day together. Maybe you could

invite one of those other voices in your head,
though. Let's plan something for next week.
You've got our number on speed dial. It's right
there between the laces. Talk to you soon, now."

Julian turned to head for the exit. He
herded Rome towards the door while repeating
"go" in his mind over and over again. The boys got
outside the house as fast as they could. Rome
looked back to see Mr. Thompson still talking to his
shoe. Correction, Mr. Thompson was talking "on"
his shoe.

Rome wondered if the confrontation with
the Garm had made Mr. Thompson crazy like that
or if he had already been a lunatic. Rome
remembered the first time he had encountered a
Garm. When Mr. Jones let him look into the portal
outside the library, and he saw what was crawling
around in The Void, Rome had become quite
anxious about his future. Perhaps being prepared
and educated on the Garms braced Rome for when
he first fought one. Or maybe, since he was a
dragon, he was more mentally stable when it came
to interacting with Darkbrands. Either way, he felt
pity for Mr. Thompson. Garms were truly hideous
nether-beasts. Confronting one alone in the dark
just might drive someone mad.

The boys quickly fled to the safety of the driveway and beyond to the street. They walked a few houses down to where a streetlight provided them with some solace. Rome sat down on the curb while Julian tossed his die up in the air a few times.

"So, what do we do?' asked Rome. "It is nighttime, and I do not think we can see much in the woods at night. I mean, I can, but you would be blind out there."

"Time to contact Mr. Jones and get us outta here," said Julian. He whipped out his iPad which still had the Candy Crush logo on it. He sent a text message to Mr. Jones's number asking for them to be "extracted from Looneyville and put back in their dormitory".

In a flash, the boys were standing back in their room. Julian laid down on his bed and started tossing his die up in the air again. Rome walked over to the phone and quickly dialed Mr. Jones at the library. The phone rang several times with no answer. Rome hung up and tried again with the same result.

"I get no answer," said Rome.

"Oh, well," said Julian. "There's nothing we can do tonight anyway. I memorized that crackpot's address. We can see if Mr. Jones can drop us there again tomorrow, and we can make a trek through the woods. We may be coming upon our first evidence of a portal, man. Better be ready with that dragon fire!"

"And you better be ready with those iron skillets and twigs," replied Rome.

"Dude," said Julian. "I've got something extra special up my chainmail sleeve for this one. You're gonna love this, bro!" Julian put himself into a fit of laughter and rolled around on his bed.

Rome was worried. Had a combination of Titus S. Thompson's psychosis and Camela Rider's Napoleonic Complex rubbed off on his partner? He would find out tomorrow.

Chapter Nine

The next morning, Rome woke Julian up forcibly in order for the boys to be ready for roll call. Julian had stayed up late doing who knows what. Most likely, he was either watching skateboarding videos or preparing for an impending battle. Those were the extremes of Julian. Rome had grown quite used to them by now. Whatever he had been doing, Rome could guarantee that he was laser focused on the endeavor. Julian's determination and attention to detail were truly on point.

The day went by fast. Before Rome could blink, it was lunch time. After his second blink, they were being released for the day. A quick check of the watch let Rome know that they had about four hours until sundown. That should be plenty of time to investigate the campsite and look for portal evidence.

Mr. Jones was waiting for them in the "comfortable" chair when they arrived in their dorm room. Luckily, Rome had packed them up with some snacks and provisions for the expedition before school that day. The boys lined up and waited for Mr. Jones to teleport them back to Mr. Thompson's house. Mr. Jones began his Transportation Incantation and zapped the boys across the city at a molecular level.

Both Rome and Julian were excited and nervous at the same time. They had seen a lot in the last few months. They had seen strange monsters from the ranks of an evil armada. They had seen people visibly affected by the ever impending war between worlds. They had seen an unlikely trio of determined advocates come together to protect their planet. What they DIDN'T see was Camela Rider walk through the dorm room door just in time to see them flicker and vanish out of sight. She stood there for a second, and then firmly placed her tiny hands on her hips and groaned like a frustrated toddler.

Just like before, the boys appeared by the driveway to Mr. Thompson's home. They scouted the house for a few moments to see if there was any movement inside, but they could not see any signs of its resident. Perhaps he went jellybean shopping with his mum after all.

Riders of Fire and Ice

Julian fired up the spatial linking.

"We need to get to the backyard"

"Okay, Jules. Follow me."

Rome tiptoed to the side of the house and flattened himself up against the fence that ran along the neighbor's yard. As quietly as he could, Rome shuffled all the way down the fence to where the property dividing line ended and the woods began behind Mr. Thompson's house

"I wish we could go invisible like the Garms," said Rome across the spatial linking.

"At least we don't smell as bad as them, bro."

"That's one way I can always tell if there is one near. My dragon nose picks up on a lot of stuff."

"Your powers are wicked awesome. You think we'll get to use them today?" Julian was ramping up.

"I hope not. My wish is that we have no fights with Garms today. Are you ready to make a dash for the wood line?"

"Do it to it, dude!"

The boys ran as swiftly as they could from the edge of the neighbor's yard to the entrance of the woods. The shrubbery had overgrown so much that there was little chance Mr. Thompson would see them out his back windows. The boys wanted to take every precaution to avoid detection though. Mr. Thompson DID have a very intimidating shotgun after all.

Once inside the cover of the woods, the boys slowed to a fast-paced walk. Navigating through the unknown woods was hard, but they made rapid progress. Julian's iPad provided them with a compass so they knew they were heading in the right direction. Straight back until they reached a rock wall. Then, head east until they reached the lake. Simple directions.

Pretty soon the boys made it to the rock wall. It was about ten feet high with all manner of vines and tree roots growing out of it. Even with all those protrusions, it seemed nearly impossible to climb. As for the length of the thing, it extended well beyond sight (even dragon sight) into the woods in both directions.

The boys headed east towards where the

lake should be with mild trepidation. They tried to make small talk, but each one literally knew what the other was thinking. They were moments away from possibly coming upon another portal. Another enemy. That meant battle. That meant danger.

Just like Mr. Thompson said, the woods emptied out into a clearing with a gorgeous view of the lake. The lake itself was not huge by any means. It was wide enough to boat across, but one could easily swim it as well. It was murky which made guessing the depth hard. There were beige, sandy beaches outlining most of its border which held fragile and diverse ecosystems. Bird calls came from the trees, and swarms of insects harmonized a blanketing chorus as the boys walked towards the shoreline. Rome even spied a striped-neck terrapin slide itself into the muddy water, and he heard fish jump in the distance. The lake was quaint, much like the town that it bordered.

"Look down there," said Julian aloud.

Rome looked to where Julian pointed and saw the wreckage of Mr. Thompson's campsite. Even from fifty feet away, the boys could make out the destroyed tent and the remnants of a deserted campfire. Rome could still smell the smoldered embers and ashen wood with his dragon nose even though it had been months since Mr. Thompson's visit. The campsite had definitely been deserted in a hurry.

"We should check it out, and then we can look around for portals," said Rome.

"I'll have my die ready just in case," responded Julian.

The boys walked down to the water's edge near the abandoned site. The place was a wreck. It clearly seemed like a Garm had ripped through the place. The tent was completely annihilated with most of it shredded to ribbons. The wood from the fire pit was thrown all over the place. There was a book bag whose contents were strewn across the lake shore like trash on a highway. It was a calamity!

"Well, this is a cluster," said Julian. "Let's check the water and see if there's any nasty, black and purple hair floating in it."

The boys walked closer to the edge of the lake. They could not see the bottom because of all the grass and muck clogging the view. The water looked like it was both constantly and freshly disturbed.

Rome was anxious because he could smell and feel the presence of a Darkbrand. Something had been here more recently than the original attack last winter. It was a possibility that it had been here within the past day or two. Rome knew that smell far too well. It was a stench beyond all stenches. Something inside Rome was tugging at him. It was like he had a sixth sense, and it was trying to alert him to something. He could feel the awareness screaming its warning on a cellular level. Something was not right here.

"Move!" Rome shouted unexpectedly. He grabbed the back of Julian's hoodie and yanked him back from the edge.

A giant figure shot out of the water and landed five feet from where the boys were standing. It stood on two legs with its back to them. Slowly, it turned a massive head and leaned down to get a closer look at them. Rome swallowed hard. Julian had been inches away from being skewered by a Minotaur erupting from the lake.

Now this was a REAL beast from The Void. The half man half bull was a nightmarish sight to behold. It stood nearly ten monstrous feet tall and probably weighed half a ton of pure, angry muscle. It had sturdy hooves for feet and bear-like claws for hands. Its head contained two large horns which stuck out symmetrically over its eyes, and they were probably a good three feet long themselves. It had clearly visible white scars along its face and shoulders attesting to its history of bloodshed. This Minotaur was obviously battle hardened. All over its powerful body was dark blue fur which seemed to repel the water from the lake. For cover, a green loincloth hung tied around its waist which offered superb flexibility, but not much protection. Lastly, a long, sinuous tail whipped back and forth between the monster's goliath legs.

It peered at the boys as if somewhat stunned to find them there. Satisfied they were no threat, it huffed heavy, raunchy breath in the boys' faces three or four times before rearing its head back and letting out a thunderous roar. Intending mortal harm, it raised its arms above its head and brought them down like an axe-handle smash.

Milliseconds before the Minotaur's unforgiving fists came smashing down into the earth, the boys jumped out of the way. Almost out of instinct, Rome let out a fire flash from his eyes which gave the boys enough time to regroup twenty feet away from the monster.

"OOOohmagosh! Ooooohmagosh! We are in it for real," said Julian. "That's one serious looking adversary, dude! I don't think we are ready for something like this!"

"I doubt we can convince it to reschedule, Jules," exclaimed Rome.

In fact, the Minotaur was far from interested. It sneezed away Rome's fire attack and stared at the boys with a bloodthirsty look on its face. It clenched its fists intermittently and snarled violently at them as if it's temper had just been jacked up significantly. That's when Rome noticed something that made his stomach turn.

"Hey, Jules," he whimpered. "Check out its left horn."

Julian looked up to see that approximately two inches of the tip of the monster's left horn looked to be missing. It appeared to have been cut cleanly off as if by a laser. Julian reached into his pocket and pulled out the piece of bone they had found when they sealed the portal at their school. He didn't even need to check it. Both boys knew it was a perfect fit.

"Uh-oh!" said Julian.

The Minotaur took notice of the fragment Julian held in his hand. It let out another fuming roar and pounded the terrain crossly. It set its hands on the ground and fiercely kicked its hind leg against the dirt preparing a charge attack. And then, it charged them.

"Julian!" Rome shouted. "Toss that bone chip! And then toss your die!"

Julian threw the piece of horn as far into the lake as he could. The Minotaur veered away from its original targets and dove straight into the lake to retrieve its missing body part. The boys took this time to retreat further up the beach towards the woods. They dug in behind an old log and watched the lake for any kind of movement. Julian pulled out his magical die and showed it to Rome.

"Are you ready, brother?" asked Julian.

Before Rome could answer, there was another loud commotion coming from the lake edge. The Minotaur popped back out of the water and surveyed the beach for the boys. After several guttural grunts of frustration, the Minotaur began its task at hand. The boys watched as it re-attached the bone bit to its horn. From somewhere deep in the woods, two or three black, gaseous masses zoomed to the general vicinity of the Minotaur. They swirled around its head like a smoke-filled blender. After a pixelating flash, the dark nebulae dissipated and the horn appeared as good as new. Fully completed, the Minotaur scoured the beach for its enemies again.

This time, however, he would be facing off against a fire dragon from the Den of Volcana and a bloodline descendent of the first Synergist Knight. Julian rolled the die which landed on one. They made their transformations into dragon and knight and prepared for their enemy. Over the last few months, they had been discussing battle strategies with Mr. Jones. Now, they had synchronized attack plans and coordinated schemes in place. Plus they had the advantage of being able to use the spatial linking. Should be easy, right?

Rome turned to face the Minotaur approximately fifty feet away. He spread his wings and stood up on his hind legs to make himself look intimidating. He even let out a mythical howl to threaten it. Julian, now dressed in full knight regalia, ran out from behind the log in order to flank the Minotaur on its left side. He took cover behind a pile of large stones and aimed his magical bow, Artemis, at the side of the Minotaur's head.

The Minotaur, not to be out maneuvered began a slow approach towards the dragon. The ground vibrated under each hooved step the monster took. From a sheath on its back, it pulled out a grueling and sinister looking war hammer. Much like the Minotaur itself, its weapon appeared to be quite top heavy. The head of the hammer was nearly a foot in diameter with multitudes of hieroglyphic-like etchings on the body. The fore-end of the haft had an extremely dangerous spike that was about fifteen inches in length. The hammer's shaft was so long that it took both hands to carry the gruesome device. This projected to be an epic battle indeed.

Rome took one look at the weapon and decided he did not want to make this a close quarter's fight. He began unloading on the lumbering giant with streams of red-hot fire. At first, the Minotaur was able to withstand the attacks, but as it got closer, it had to start dodging Rome's fire breath. The constant moving made it impossible for Julian to get a clean shot with his magical bow. He moved from his position to the rear of the Minotaur as it got ever closer to Rome. He immediately regretted this because he was now in between the Minotaur and the lake. Hopefully Rome could wound the monster enough for Artemis's silver arrows to finish it off.

Once the Minotaur got within ten feet of the fire breathing dragon, it leapt up in the air with the war hammer raised over its head. Rome had seen this attack before, but he was too big now to dodge it. Rome brought his right wing across his body like a shield to ward off the plunging strike. The Minotaur's hammer fell upon Rome's wing and bounced off. The hammer head shot down to the ground, but the Minotaur made a quick pivot and used the momentum to bring the hammer three hundred and sixty degrees around its body towards Rome's exposed chest.

Rome reacted defensively. He used his left arm's adept talons to grab the shaft of the hammer before it could crush his ribcage. The Minotaur let go of the hammer's shaft with his left hand and grabbed the right claw of Rome. The two warriors were locked into a stalemate pushing against the other with all their might.

Both struggled to get an edge in the

deadlock for a few seconds like two arm wrestlers. Rome could feel himself losing strength against the behemoth. The Minotaur's power was as relentless as it was merciless. Rome wrapped his tail around his opponent's right leg hoping to pull it out from under it. He tugged on the leg, but it was like trying to pull down a building cemented into the street. The Minotaur reacted to this ploy by head butting Rome right in the chest. Rome was punched back a few steps, and with him went his tail, so the Minotaur ended up on its back in the dirt.

However, it was up quickly and bearing down on Rome again. This time it came at Rome with its war hammer like a spear aimed at Rome's torso. Rome grabbed the head of the hammer with both claws and bore the brunt of the thrust in his side. This resulted in Rome being pushed back to the tree line where he banged up against a large pine tree. If he did not do something quickly, the tree would snap and Rome would be prone and exposed on the ground. He opened his mouth to blast the monster with a fire stream, but the Minotaur slammed its forehead into Rome's chin pinning his throat against the tree with its horns. This rendered Rome's head motionless and completely ineffective.

"Hey, Jules. How about a little help here?" yelled Rome across the spatial linking.

"I'm trying dude. I've already stuck this thing with like four arrows. I'm running out."

"Try something else. Quick! I can barely breathe!"

"I know. I feel like I'm being strangled too," complained Julian. "It's throwing off my aim. Can't you wiggle out of there? This is really uncomfortable."

Rome could see out of the corner of his eye that Julian had indeed emptied his quiver of arrows into this horrific creature. He could see five or six purple fletchings sticking out of the monster's back and shoulders. Julian was kneeling on the ground setting up to roll his die and try another one of his magical weapons. He needed to hurry. The strength of this beast was incredible. Rome could not believe how feeble he was compared to the Minotaur's brute muscle. Rome was about to be overtaken.

Suddenly, the tension in the Minotaur's grip lessened immensely. It jerked its head away from Rome's neck and let out a scream of pain. Rome gasped for precious air and shook the dizziness away. He breathed in spurts testing the capability of his flamethrower lungs in case he needed them urgently.

To Rome's surprise, his adversary had temporarily abandoned the fight. The Minotaur dropped its hammer to the ground with a clonk and whirled around to face the lake, but mostly to face its attacker. Julian could not have looked more terrified as he stood there shaking in his greaves.

Chapter Ten

Rome was panting to collect his breath while he observed what had just happened. Apparently, Julian had injured the fiend heavily. Rome looked at the leg of his foe. Stuck right in the Minotaur's freakish, left thigh was a magnificent spear. The Minotaur shrieked in pain, but also in outrage. It reached down and struggled to pull the spear from its flesh.

Although deeply imbedded in the Minotaur's ethereal muscle, Rome could still distinguish most of the splendid spear. The shaft was silver-colored, but shimmered a prismatic, rainbow as the sunlight touched it. The spear tip had grandiose wings that curved dramatically out and hooked back in like large, barbed fish hooks. At the end of the six foot shaft was a balled, iron sphere that looked cumbersome, but was undoubtedly used for balancing purposes in the hands of its wielder.

As Rome drooled over the weapon, the

Darkbrand made headway prying it out. When finally, the projectile was removed, the Minotaur went to slam the spear on the ground. However, it did not go where it was aimed. Instead, the spear flew through the air towards Julian. He reached out and caught the spear as if the motion was intended. Fearing the rage and reaction of the Minotaur, Julian clung tightly to his armament while staring it down maliciously.

"How's that sting, ya dumb ugly?" asked Julian. "I'd like you to meet my number four weapon. Gungnir! The very spear wielded by the Norse god Odin. Forged by the dwarven brethren The Sons of Ivaldi and perfected on the ancient battlefields of Valhalla. And now, ripping through your leg!"

Rome had heard of this fabled spear. He was familiar with the Norse legends including the heroic escapades of Thor and Odin. He remembered that the gods had their weaponry forged in the mountains and almost all of them had a certain, special ability ascribed to them. They were able to return to their master's hand by mental capacity alone. This meant that no matter where or how far Julian flung Gungnir, it would always come back to him like a giant, lethal boomerang. Rome could not help but be awed by such an astounding addition to Julian's arsenal. What other pleasant surprises did the young knight's die have in store for them?

The Minotaur, being less impressed, rushed Julian in a blind rage. It obviously understood English. Or maybe it just understood smack talk. It prepared to swing its war hammer right at Julian's head, but he dodged to the left and narrowly missed being flattened into oblivion.

"Get over here now, knight," roared Rome.

Julian dove to the side of his attacker and raced to join his dragon. He bravely stood in front of Rome with Gungnir steadily pointed at his foe.

"I hope you've got a plan," said Julian aloud.

"It will feel my wrath. It will burn to cinders!" Rome was obviously still ticked about the throttling he received earlier.

Rome unleashed maelstrom of fire at the Minotaur. He was using a huge amount of his reserve energy to gain them the upper hand. The Minotaur already had a wounded leg, but the fire attack should give the allies what they needed to end this battle. Rome solely based this theory on the previous encounters with Garms and being able to judge how much damage they could take.

The Minotaur shielded its face with its forearm, but was entirely engulfed by Rome's flames. With its right hand, it picked up the war hammer and stuck the shaft into ground. Something was happening to the weapon. It was glowing a strange blue aura. The lake water began to eerily creep up the shore much like a rising tide. It continued to surge and swirl around the monster's body creating a barricade of water. Rome's flames spit and sputtered becoming unable to reach his target.

After a few seconds, Rome realized his fire was not penetrating the liquid fortification, so he let up. This gave the Minotaur the opportunity it needed. The water surrounding the beast changed shape from a protective barrier to a surging spray like that of a firehose. It flew right at Rome and struck him directly inside his mouth with a the force of a tsunami.

Rome shook his head trying to get the water out of his nose and eyes. He sneezed vehemently expunging the water from his system. The sting was unbearable, and for the first time, Rome lost his cool on the battlefield. He reacted out of anger instead of responding clearly. Rome snapped his head forward and tried to irrationally spew dragon fire at his enemy. Much to his surprise, nothing came out. His attack ceased to exist. No fire came from his throat OR eyes. What was happening?

Julian spoke to him without the spatial linking. "Dragon, the water must have permeated your inner core. I'm not exactly sure how it works, but you've been dampened within. Your fire attacks have been rendered useless for now. Waste not your energy on it."

"What do we do, knight?" asked Rome. "This demon is too strong for me physically and your magical weapons are barely phasing it."

Julian shouted a war cry. "We fight on! Our line shall not break! We defend this realm! For Camelot!"

Julian put his head down and charged the Minotaur in a jousting position. Rome hovered a few feet off the ground and readied a pouncing attack. If today was to be their final day, these young warriors would not go down without a fight. Like their ancestors before them, they would be remembered in the pages of history.

Julian reached their enemy first. His spear targeted the Minotaur's upper torso. Although Julian was a very adept fighter, he was unproven with this new weapon, and the monster obviously had centuries of experience over him. It easily parried his thrusting attack and slid the shaft of its polearm down to Gungnir's spearhead which trapped it in the sand. Julian raised the butt-end of his weapon and smacked the Minotaur in its eye. This ploy only seemed to irritate the monster even more as evidenced by it trying to clip Julian with its horns. Julian let go of Gungnir and twirled behind his adversary. With a quick twitch of the wrist, Gungnir leapt to Julian's grasp and he dug the spear into the beast's back shoulder. As a counterattack, the Minotaur spun around and struck the center of Julian's chainmail with its right forearm. Julian landed nearly thirty feet away next to a large stump.

By this time, Rome was upon the monster. He batted at it with his wings and furiously swiped at it with all four claws. Though a few blows did land, the Minotaur was simply too strong for Rome even with an injured leg. It raised the end of its war hammer and drove it into Rome's chin. Rome was dazed and unable to avoid the head of the hammer as it crashed into his side with the full force of the Minotaur's swing. Rome landed close to the water's edge with portions of him lying limply in the shallows. Rome did not like water. Fitting that his demise would be directly attributed to it.

The Minotaur lurched slowly towards Rome on a hobbled leg. It grimaced and snarled at Rome disgustingly. As Rome resigned to his fate, the Minotaur lifted the lethal war hammer high above its head. The harbinger began its quick descent towards Rome's skull as he closed his dragon eyes.

Miraculously, the giant hammer did not reach Rome's head. It froze in mid-plunge grasped by a pair of snowy-white claws with gleaming talons. They pushed back against the force of the Minotaur sending it stumbling a few steps backwards. Rome, being completely exhausted, could only salvage enough strength to look up at his savior.

Standing over Rome's motionless body was ANOTHER DRAGON! It looked very much like him anatomically, but with a few vast differences. Unlike Rome, it had beautiful, white scales that shimmered in the afternoon sun. It had smaller wings than Rome, but they appeared to be made of thick, translucent crystals as opposed to leathery skin. Also, this dragon had what appeared to be a snowy mane that ran down its neck and disappeared where its shoulders met its back. The mane danced mesmerizingly even though the winds were presently no more than a delicate breeze. Rome followed the curvature of the dragon's backbone all the way down to its tail where the tip was a single, sharp spike made out of the same crystal material as its wings. It hissed venomously at the Minotaur and stood as a statuesque vision over Rome with its mane falling around them like a canopy of snowflakes . Was it protecting him?

The Minotaur rallied to roar as loud as it could and charged the guarding dragon with its war hammer ready to smash this new challenger. It swung the mighty weapon at the dragon's body, but the dragon shielded itself with those breathtaking, crystal wings. When Minotaur metal collided with plated protection, the entire lakeside rang out with a resounding, thunderous bang. In the end, the dragon's wings withstood the punishing blow of the sledge. However, the Minotaur used the same move it used on Rome and slung the hammer three hundred and sixty degrees around this time aiming at the dragon's head. The white dragon skillfully ducked underneath the attack and shoulder blocked the Minotaur in its solar plexus. While the beast was still reeling, the white dragon let lose a fury of attacks to the creature's head and neck. The dragon then gracefully skipped to the side of the monster and grabbed hold of its horns and shoulders. Then it raised its lower legs, balanced on its tail, and kicked the creature across the shore towards the water's edge.

The Minotaur slid to a stop with a face full of mud and debris. After a few seconds, it awkwardly limped to its hooves. Obviously Julian's attack was affecting it somewhat. Combined with the vicious assault from this new dragon, it seemed like the boys and their latest ally were winning the battle.

Chapter Eleven

Rome knew he had to move. He had to at least help his brother. If he could assure Julian's safety, he would double back to help the mystery dragon. He started by focusing on the spatial linking.

"Jules, can you move?" he inquired dramatically.

"I'm dead, dude. Just toss me in the lake."

"I know you are not dead, Jules. If you were dead, I would be dead. Can you move?"

"I feel like my ribs are broken. Legs seem to be functioning okay though. Where do you want me to move to? I was thinking The Bahamas?"

Before Rome could scold Julian for joking around, he was interrupted by a new voice.

"Rome of Volcana," it said. "If you are able, you must move the young knight to somewhere safe, secure, and out of the way. Make for behind the tree line."

Rome knew that voice. He had definitely heard it before somewhere. There was something about it that seemed so familiar. He couldn't put his claw on it.

Rome would have to dwell on it later because the Minotaur was gathered and readying for another confrontation. It stuck the shaft of its war hammer into the shore again and began channeling the water into the surge attack that had incapacitated Rome's dragon fire. The water swirled around the Minotaur and shot at the white dragon in six separate liquid missiles. They flew fast and on target as if they were guided by their creator.

The white dragon enveloped itself with its wings creating a fractal fortification. The water projections slammed hard into the dragon but froze on contact. They solidified into chunks of ice and shattered into millions of pieces all over the beach.

Rome used this distraction to rise to his feet and make for his partner. He was slowed by multiple injuries, including broken ribs and internal water damage. He did take a moment to glance back at the battle. The Minotaur was sending wave after wave of water blasts at the dragon. Each attack resulted in the same fate. Once they struck the white dragon's wings, they froze and exploded into ice cubes. The problem was that those very ice shards were being deflected all over the beach, and coming dangerously close to Julian's exposed body. To make matters worse, the Minotaur had an unlimited supply of ammunition as it was using the water from the lake for its enchanted bullets. Rome would have to get back into the fight as soon as possible.

But first, he needed to get Julian away from the front line and to the safety of the woods. Rome's mouth had been damaged by the hydrant attack so he continued to use his spatial linking even though they now seemed to have been hacked by another user. Whose voice was that? How did it know Rome's name?

"Jules, do you still have possession of your spear?"

"Yes, but I would rather have possession of a full body cast."

"Just stick it up in the air and hold on tight. I will swing by and grab you before you get hit by shrapnel."

"Come and get me, bro," sighed Julian

Rome slinked towards his fallen comrade as fast as his injured body could go. Ice spikes were landing all around him. Most were too small to do any serious damage, but every now and then a large one would stab into the ground in Rome's path to his brother. Rome was hoping he could get to Julian before he got skewered by one of the frozen, falling stalactites.

Rome saw Julian waving Gungnir pathetically in the air like a veritable white flag. His eyes were shut, but he was smirking mischievously. He tried to laugh as Rome approached, but fell into a coughing spell. Rome was curious as to what Julian was up to.

"What is so funny, Jules?" probed Rome over their spatial linking.

"You mean you don't recognize the voice in our spatial linking? I think it's hilarious. Think blonde, strong, and always talks in threes."

"WHAT???? No way, Jules! You have got to be kidding me! Hold on!"

Rome grabbed hold of Gungnir with his left claw and trotted to the tree line. His ravaged ribs throbbed, but he was able to deposit Julian out of harm's way near a couple of tall bushes. He glanced down at Julian and used the spatial linking again.

"You do not really think...."

The other voice interrupted Rome's train of thought.

"Knight, you must relinquish the Norse God's spear, cover yourself with the English King's shield, and stay quiet. Rome of Volcana, you are hurt. Stay with your brother. We will handle this demon. You must rest, heal up, and not interfere."

"We? Who is WE???" demanded Rome

Before Rome got a response, the white dragon opened its wings and launched itself at the Minotaur. It flew just above the Minotaur's head and wrapped its tail around the creature's neck and horn. Then it landed behind its foe and catapulted the blue-haired beast fifty feet across the beach.

Before the Minotaur could get fully to its feet, the white dragon was attacking again. This time it got down on all fours, tucked in its wings, and attempted to stab the brute with its echinated, tail spike. The Minotaur defended itself against the onslaught with its war hammer which gave off brilliant sparks and fire each time the weapons crossed. It was clear the white dragon gained a decided advantage as the Minotaur became increasingly defensive.

At last, the dragon landed a critical blow, piercing the Minotaur's left shoulder with its tail. The Minotaur yowled hellishly and pushed the dragon away with the haft of its hammer. In a last ditch effort, the Minotaur dug its weapon into the dirt and called upon the lake water to create another encircling barrier. The white dragon, wise to this ploy, jumped back so as not to be upended by the swirling liquid shield. Again, it enclosed itself in its wings.

Then, something strange happened. The Minotaur sniffed the air as if trying to locate another adversary. Clouds formed in a circle around its head inside the water defense. They changed from a wispy haze into thick, dark storm clouds. In a matter of moments, there began a rancorous downfall of heavy snow surrounding the Minotaur. Seconds later, the snow became a miniature blizzard collapsing on the Minotaur and blinding it.

The Minotaur let out a silent scream inside its cage and wrenched its neck wildly trying to fight off the storm with its horns. Since it was completely blinded by the blizzard and hindered by wounds, the monster lost its balance and fell to the dirt. Once again, it swung its horns around at its ethereal assailant and grunted mucoid discharge from its nostrils. With feverous anger, it raged and punched the cold air encompassing it.

The Minotaur reached another level of energy output by throwing back its head and howling tremendously. The blizzard dissipated under the force of the invigorated water magic. Its hydraulic defense system churned around the monster at an increasing pace, and expanded outward at least a couple feet. It was now a seething, surging aura of water energy about to be released on the Minotaur's challenger.

As the Minotaur continued to raise a tidal wave around it, the white dragon peeked out from the crystalline shelter. It cocked its head slightly and then unleashed a freezing stream of wintry breath at the Minotaur. The attack was similar to Rome's except it was an icy blast instead of fire. The breath overwhelmed the Minotaur's barricade and began freezing the water into solid ice. In a matter of moments, the entire defense system was frozen through and the Minotaur was encased in a sub-zero prison. The evil being had caused its own demise, and it would never again draw breath in this realm.

The white dragon, satisfied with its handiwork, slowly opened its wings. To Rome's utter shock, a child-sized human exited the enclosure and walked over to the newly formed ice sculpture. Rome recognized the hair and frail physique immediately. A pig-tailed girl walked around the masterpiece tapping on the ice with a small scepter. One end appeared crescent-shaped like a thin moon sliver, and the other, shaped like an ornate decoration, had a brilliant, blue crystal lodged in its center. As for the pint-sized pugilist, she wore the tiniest and shiniest suit of plate mail Rome had ever seen. It barely made a sound when she moved and twinkled as if dusted with glitter. She stopped in front of the beast and twirled her baton a couple times before striking the frozen monster in the chest area. The Minotaur shattered into a million tiny pieces of ice which danced musically on the lake shore sand.

Rome could barely believe his dragon eyes

when Camela Rider looked over at the boys and spoke in her shrill and viperous voice.

"How disappointed you must feel to require a rescue," she mocked. "I expected more from the Den of Volcana". She sighed and looked at her scepter as if in profound contemplation. "What now, fool brother? What now, indeed?"

Chapter Twelve

The white dragon met Camela on the lakeshore. It lowered its head to the ground and allowed Camela to step onto it. Once aboard, it elevated its head so that Camela slid down its neck to the crux of its shoulders. The white dragon started towards the boys at a moderate pace, and Camela chastised them as the duo approached.

"I must say, boys. You shall be counting your blessings this evening that my Master Dragon and I happened upon you in this dejected state. Had we not intervened, you would both have fallen victim to one of the Hydrotaur Generals." Camela motioned for the white dragon to stop so she could jump off. "Had my opinion won the day, you both would be smashed to smithereens right now. You may thank the nobility from Iglacia that you still have your skins."

Nobility from Iglacia? An actual ice dragon? Another dragon in the flesh? Or scales? Rome was hardly able to contain his exuberance behind his toothy smile.

Julian coughed in pain. "Dang, Camela. You're so wrapped up in your egotism that you would have let your own brother die? That's messed up, man!"

Camela looked into her scepter again. "To perish on the battlefield is the greatest glory The House of Rider can attain." She looked back at Julian. "Of course, I jest. I would only have you suffer a tad more."

Rome looked at Julian grabbing his ribs and trying to sit up. "Oh good. I thought she was gonna say she would let me croak. We cannot choose our family, can we, dragon?"

Julian rolled his magic die between his hands. "I hate to have to change you back, dragon, but we are fiercely injured and require healing." He reached up and touched the side of Rome's face. "I'm proud of what you did today, and I thank you for saving my life." Julian let the die fall to the dirt. As was intended, it landed on one. The Great Synergy flash surrounded the boys, and they were instantaneously reverted back to their non-combatant selves; totally healed and totally mundane.

"The stars are aligning," said Camela. "Now I understand why you struggled so mightily with that Hydrotaur. You relied on the Hope of Pandora to perform The Great Synergy. You've cheated. You have not performed The Great Synergy to its fullest extent. One more letdown to add to the litany of your shortcomings, brother."

Julian had heard enough. He advanced swiftly on his bratty, little sister, but the white dragon snaked its head between the two siblings and flashed its teeth in Julian's face. Julian shoved the dragon on its nose and stood in front of his sister with his arms crossed.

"What do you know about Pandora's Hope? Or The Great Synergy? Or ANY of this?" He pointed angrily at the white dragon. "Have you bonded with a dragon, Camela??? Dad's gonna freaking kill you!!!"

"And what of you, Julian?" she interjected. "What if father were to find out about your transgressions? Would you not face similar castigation? It seems our situation obliges we keep one another's secrets less we fall out of father's good graces. Necessity makes for strange bedfellows, as they say."

Julian chewed on his lip. "Fine! But I've got some questions for you," he stated robustly.

"Fair enough, you dunce!" moaned Camela. "But first, allow me to get more comfortable. Even a Lady from The House of Rider can be chafed by Valkyrie armor." She moved over to her dragon and caressed the side of its face. She whispered at a level that was barely audible. "I'm sorry, my sister. I know you much prefer your true form, but for all four of us to converse coherently, we require an avenue of communication shared by all."

The white dragon sighed slightly creating a waft of freezing air. Rome neared the white dragon and studied it. He had only seen himself in the glass of their lunchroom once. Now was his time to actually see what a dragon looked like from a first-hand perspective. He felt a connection to this dragon, being one himself. He understood why it preferred to be in this form with all the freedom it provided. The feeling of being trapped in his skin constantly rivaled the desire to be unbridled and flying free like he knew he should be. Rome wondered to himself if this dragon felt the same way? He wondered if this dragon dealt with the same stresses and dilemmas of being a dragon stuck in a human world.

Camela, still rubbing the white dragon's face, closed her eyes. She stepped back, and in a white flash of brilliance, she was back in her school uniform. As the boys expected, Krysta now stood next to her. Her hair still danced in the breeze just like the mane of her dragon form. Krysta smiled at the boys and waved innocently. She, too was back in her school uniform complete with her blue and white motif. Now, it all made sense to the boys.

"I am sorry for harnessing your spatial linking," she said. "It is not a common practice, but I needed to communicate with, alert, and direct you. I am truly sorry." She stared at the ground.

The boys looked at each other. Rome remembered that Mr. Jones had told them that the spatial linking allowed other Synergy users to also utilize the telepathy the boys shared. He had mentioned that entire sects of the resistance army were able to communicate on the battlefield with this wondrous technique. Krysta was certainly advanced if she was able to apply her own thoughts to the boys' channel.

Rome spoke up. "It is no big deal, Krysta. Honestly, you probably saved our lives by doing that. Please do not worry about it."

She looked at Rome almost trembling. "As you know, one of the side effects of spatial linking is that the user accesses the innovator's thoughts and feelings. So, by pirating your link, I unintentionally was exposed to, admitted to, and subjected to both of your consciences and sub-consciences. It is an unfortunate invasion of privacy. I deeply rue, regret, and apologize for it."

Julian wrinkled his nose and scratched his cheek. "In that case," he said. "Let ME apologize to YOU! I feel terrible for you to have entered that depraved world. Seriously, Krysta, don't worry about it. It was necessary, and we thank you for doing it. I feel bad because you may never sleep again!"

"Uggggh," Camela groaned. "Who knows what vile debauchery my sister has been exposed to?" She threw her hands in the air. "Krysta and I will remedy that illness when it rears its ugly head. For now, methinks we must compare information. We have questions regarding your intentions here, and you MUST have questions for us. Conversely, the sun appears close to its submission. We shall want for a fire before long. Perhaps the dragon of Volcana can assist us."

The four of them quickly made a pile of dried logs near Mr. Thompson's original fire pit, and Rome lit it with his eye fires. They sat close to the heat with the intent of exchanging information. Rome was intrigued by the girls now more than ever. Krysta was another dragon! He had a million questions he wanted to ask her, but the humans did most of the talking first.

"So, that was a Minotaur we fought, huh?" asked Julian. "One of the Hydrotaur generals of the Darkbrand army?"

"Yes," said Camela. "Of course, you recall from your studies that there are six separate factions of elemental Minotaurs. Each militia (water, forest, earth, wind, fire, and ice) has five generals at all given times. If one general were to perish in battle, the next most formidable one would replace it. They are the leaders of the raid parties on our realm and organized packs of Garms during war.

Camela pondered for a moment. "In fact, it is rather odd that there was only a lone Minotaur here without his adorning squadron. Perhaps he lost them in the woods." Rome and Julian exchanged glances, and Julian made a zip your lips motion. "Either way, it appears we accomplished the feat of destroying one Minotaur general this eve. I shall document this victory in my battle log with the side note that our opponent was a tough nut to crack."

Julian ignored her awful pun. "Well, if we can't stop the army, at least we can force them to reshuffle their hierarchy!" Julian punched Rome in the shoulder laughing.

"A small victory for a small mind," sighed Camela.

Julian brushed off the comment. "Camela," he said. "Let's move on to the elephant in the room. Where did you find a dragon? It took me and Mr. Jones years to find one."

"I found her online in a chatroom about fantasy cosplay," she replied nonchalantly. "Next question?"

"Wait. What?" said Julian in a high pitched voice. "You found a dragon in human form ONLINE?"

"Of course not, moron," snapped Camela. "She was in her true form. Apparently, even the dragons in hiding have internet capability these days. Krysta was raised to know the true history like you and me, but she believes in the coexistence of races and the reemergence. She rebelled against her family's desire to stay in seclusion and searched out a companion to bond with."

"But how does she stay in human form?" cried Julian. "Rome did not even know he was a dragon. It was a concealment spell placed on his family like a curse. Did Krysta have the same thing?"

"No, Sir Julian," replied Krysta. "My family lived in the freezing north hidden from the humans. I have enjoyed my true form most of my life. It was not until recently that I learned the workings of human magic, spells, and enchantments."

Camela barged in. "I found a concealment spell in Father's garage to help facilitate our alliance. Now, as we are sisters, we are free to investigate the evil leaking into our world. Next question?"

"Why did you leave you den?" prodded Julian.

"Let us just say that ice dragons have a way

of being literally frozen in their ways," laughed Krysta. "And they carry grudges indefinitely. My mother, father, and sister claimed the only way we could survive was by staying as far away from humans as we could. My parents knew the tales of how our kind were hunted and maltreated after the Despot War, and they did not want that for their daughters. But I was curious, and rebellious, and determined."

Rome felt a warmth inside him. There WERE other dragons! Krysta mentioned an entire family of ice dragons. Maybe there were more of his kind as well. This was the most important discovery the boys had made yet.

Rome spoke up shyly. "Krysta, do you not find it difficult to keep your true identity a secret?"

She looked deep into Rome's eyes. "It is not easy. I find this form rather restricting, confining, and surprisingly itchy. However, I know the consequences should I be caught in my true form. Both my sister and I would be judged, persecuted, and possibly imprisoned. We both know what a permanent separation would result in. A life without my sworn sister is no life at all, so we fight our war in secret, shadow, and costume. It is my sacrifice."

"Yeah, yeah, yeah," said Julian. "I get that. Free the dragons and all, but how did this happen? How did you perform The Great Synergy?"

"Through the use of my Talisman, of course!" barked Camela. She shot a glance at Julian's die. "Wait, have you just recently realized your Talisman's immense properties?" She chuckled and snorted in a sudden fit of laughter. "Perhaps you should read the transcripts a little more closely instead of skimming through them so you can watch soccer. Doest thou not remember the teachings father imparted on us from the texts?"

Julian stared blankly as if looking right through his sister.

Camela groaned and pulled a book from her bag. It was hand-sized and bound in red leather with black and silver font. Rome had seen one like it before. Camela handed it to Rome's outstretched hands, and he recognized its similarity immediately. It looked just like the book Mr. Jones had used when instructing the boys back in Georgia. He read the title to himself, "Reemergence: The Talismans". Rome breathed out slowly realizing there were more manuscripts than originally anticipated by his posse.

Rome looked at Julian earnestly. Julian picked his ear. "There is more to this than we know! Pay attention, Jules."

Chapter Thirteen

Rome read the book to his partner while the girls talked on the other side of the fire. He skipped the stuff they already knew about The First and The Tyrant King. Mr. Jones had driven the ancient history parts into their heads, but this book provided better details of the events during The Despot War. Rome found that Julian's ancestor, the stable boy, and his dragon friend had performed The Great Synergy not by accident or out of necessity like the boys had. They had actually performed a ritual like The First and The Tyrant King; and they had used a Talisman.

According to the book, there were many magical devices on Earth. Certain ones could do amazing things. Certain ones could do less than extraordinary things. The last few pages of the book described some of these magical objects. Rome stared in disbelief at the plethora of information contained within.

"Hey," chimed in Julian reading over Rome 's

shoulder. "There's the section about Pandora's Hope. Read it to me," he demanded. Rome did as directed.

> **Pandora's Die of Hope**- According to the Greek parable, when Pandora let all of the evil into the world, she found Hope at the bottom of the box. The physical representation of "hope" is a die that is able to be imbued with powerful weapons to fight the evil existing in our realm. At the time, the Greeks were the most powerful society in the world, so she inserted The Caduceus into it hoping its healing ability would remedy the damage she had created. Over the centuries, more rulers have placed their divine weapons into the Die of Hope to both cement their legacies and help future generations battle malevolent forces. Included are:
>
> The Roman Gods put in the bow and arrows Artemis blessed with the ability to always hit its target.
>
> The Norse Gods put in Odin's spear, Gungnir, with its magic ability to return to its wielder when thrown.

Camelot's King Arthur put in his shield, Pridwen. It is impervious to all elemental attacks.

The Scottish, rebel warlord William Wallace put in his great sword, Claymore, and its ability to cut through any material.

The Dragon dens of The Despot War imbued the die with the ability to replicate The Great Synergy. It is only a replication not the true ritual thus limiting its users.

Pandora put in The Caduceus. Its healing factor would help injured warriors during their battles.

Rome looked at Julian in amazement. "That explains so much," he said.

"Yeah. I can't wait to use my giant, kick-ass sword, dude!"

Rome decided to not comment on Julian's silliness. "No, I mean about how we performed The Great Synergy. The die's version is only a replication of the true ritual. We did not do it the right way." He turned back to Camela. "So, how were YOU able to perform The Great Synergy?"

"We used this," she replied. She held up her scepter and pointed to a large blue jewel fastened to one end of the royal mace. The weapon itself was a silver and gray scepter about three feet long with a bladed-sickle on one end. The end that housed the precious stone was shaped like a snowflake with several sharp points coming off it in a spiral design. The jewel on the end caught Rome's eye immediately. Upon closer inspection, Rome could see assortments of white and silver sparkles twinkling throughout the gem. They moved around the surface like microscopic organisms on a petri dish.

"This is the Forstshard," she said proudly. "It is the Talisman responsible for our symbiotic union and my weapon of choice for the slaying of Darkbrands!"

Rome flipped through a couple of pages until he found a picture of the beautiful, aquamarine gem and an accompanying description.

> **The Frostshard-** During the germinal days of life on Earth, a meteor struck near the northern, arctic area. It consisted of an unknown, alien material similar to Earth's

diamond. Only three rock-like pieces survived the crash (the rest froze and broke in the icy temperatures). Nocturns attempted to manipulate these fragments, but accidentally set off an enormous blizzard which modern man called The Ice Age. Fearing the stones' awesome power, they were discarded into a volcano where they merged into one indestructible gemstone. After eons, the volcano cooled, and the stone was reformed into the current configuration. The unrelenting power had been stunted by chemical transformations during its time inside. Finally, it was discovered again by human rulers of the North. Its ability to create temporary snowstorms and miniature blizzards make for a divine weapon in the right hands.

Camela continued. "Father gave me this heirloom on my eleventh birthday, and I immediately knew my destiny called for me to become a Synergist Knight. From that day forward, I scoured my world in hopes of finding a willing partner to bond with. Thanks to Krysta, I have realized my vocation, and now, I am the great savior of The House of Rider. That includes saving your worthless hide, Julian."

"I'm sure you'll never let me live that one down, dear sister," mocked Julian. "It's true you saved our lives, but you also destroyed the only lead we had. We came out here following up on a Garm encounter; we locked horns with a Minotaur, and now, we're sitting here twiddling our thumbs. All thanks to The Frostshard and freezer breathe over there."

Camela glared angrily at her older brother. "Krysta has forfeited much to join me in my objective. She has voluntarily abandoned her family and her home. She has renounced a life of safety and refuge to aid me on this perilous quest. She has even given up her own TRUE FORM for my crusade. Her sacrifices are selfless and considerable. What have you done, clown, besides drop a die and stumble upon one of Earth's most important mysteries?"

"Hey," proclaimed Julian. "I have done a lot for this cause. I had to leave the majority of my video games at home to make this little trip. Also, I have now gone three whole days without watching extreme sports on a big-screen television." Julian pondered for a second. "And don't even get me started on the last five years of being stuck with

Mr. Jones."

"Prithee, who is Mr. Jones?" doubted Camela.

"Never mind," sighed Julian too mentally exhausted to even call him an old fogey.

Rome, who had been reading steadily in the new book jumped up suddenly. He whirled around to face Julian. "I think I got us a new lead," he cheered. With one hand in the air, he read the following aloud.

> **Fujin's Teardrop-** Fujin is the immortal, Japanese god of the wind. It was said that when he was born, his breath spread all the clouds so that the sun and heaven shined down upon the Earth. The sight was so beautiful that he cried a single tear that plummeted to our realm. That supernatural teardrop was claimed by humans which instilled in them the ability to ride the winds and air currents. Its essence is kept in an orb which emits a vermillion light when in use. This was one of the first Talismans weaponized by mankind and has been attributed to several historical wars throughout history.

"That's great that you are keeping up with ancient, cultural deities, bro," said Julian. "But how in the world does that help us?"

"Seriously?" asked Rome. "Do you not remember the female silhouette that has been stalking us?"

Julian looked at Rome vacantly.

"The shadow that flies around with the glowing, red orb draped around its neck?" tried Rome.

Julian turned his head slightly and breathed through his mouth.

Rome let out an exasperated sigh. He faced the girls. "I believe our chaperone and principal, Mrs. Case, may be in possession of this Talisman. There is a strange shadow that has been following me around lately, and I think it's her. She has constantly escaped me by gliding away at superhuman speeds or watching us in crowded places where I cannot transform to engage."

"Oh yeah!" laughed Julian smacking himself on the forehead with his palm.

"Hmmmm," pondered Krysta. "If you feel

strongly that this Mrs. Case is somehow in ownership of one of the Talismans, I would highly suggest, advise, and implore that we find out as much information as we can about her. Since it is unknown if she is friend or foe, and she may wield the power of Fujin's Teardrop, we may need to confront, interrogate, and contain her."

"A solid plan, Krysta," said Camela. "As usual, you provide the perfect balance of a valiant warrior and a sagacious tactician. We shall pursue this course, but first we must adhere to the calls of nature and rest our mortal instruments."

"Uuuuuuugh," groaned Julian. "Can you just speak like a normal person for once? Is that too much to ask? It's so confusing when you talk like that."

"Okay, Julian," replied Camela. "Let us see if you can decipher THIS vernacular." She moved closer to Krysta who suddenly converted into her ice dragon form. Camela jumped onto Krysta's head and slid down her neck. Then, she spun to face the boys in her shiny Valkyrie armor.

"Good luck getting home," she spat. Then, she stuck her tiny tongue out at the boys and spurred Krysta into the air.

Riders of Fire and Ice

Krysta created a tremendous downwind as she flew away from the makeshift campfire. The boys covered their faces to avoid the sand and soot from flying into their eyes. Julian shook his fist at the departing duo and yelled some cruel words that were drowned out by the vacating dragon. Then he threw a stick at them. He missed.

Krysta's voice came over the spatial linking. "Rome, get some rest tonight. After school tomorrow, we will meet up, deliberate a plan, and speak with Mrs. Case. Be prepared. I hope tonight's events have not changed what you think of me. I cherish the idea, possibility, and promise of us sharing so much in the future. As dragons in a human world, there is much to gain, obtain, and learn from each other. Pleasant dreams, Rome from Volcana."

"And the same to you, Krysta of Iglacia."

"I will see YOU in my dreams."

Rome turned a shade of red that rivaled his scales. Julian laughed out loud and pointed at Rome. "You have ANOTHER stalker! This one is of the dragon variety!"

"Do NOT be jealous, Jules!" said Rome.

Riders of Fire and Ice

Rome grabbed Julian's wrist and pushed some buttons on his watch/phone. It rang a couple times, and Rome lifted it to his mouth. "Mr. Jones," he said. "Pull us out. We are done here. We are coming home with some major updates and a few new bruises."

The boys flickered in and out a couple times and then vanished into thin air with Julian still guffawing. The beach was desolate now, and the moon shined brightly on the lake shore. The treacherous Minotaur was banished from this place, and the boys were safe. Nonetheless, about one hundred yards into the forest, there was another wickedness stirring on a massive tree that stood alone in a small clearing. The tree looked completely normal at first glance. However, to the trained eye, there was one minute difference between it and the other trees in the forest. On the backside of the tree was a gnarled knoll that housed all manner of insects and a few birds' nests. Etched into this knoll was a very disturbing insignia from Rome and Julian's recent past. In a language too old for humans to read was the foreboding, shimmering symbol for portal. And just on the other side of this emblem were hordes of malevolent Darkbrands seething to break through the threshold.

Chapter Fourteen

The next day of school absolutely flew by for the boys and the girls. The plan was to meet at the boys' dorm room and then, as a foursome, blindside Mrs. Case in her dormitory. Regardless of Mrs. Case's allegiance, or lack of, they would need to be on their highest guard. Anyone in possession of one of the Talismans should not be taken lightly.

Of course, the idea that Mrs. Case had one of the Talismans was all predicated on Rome's assumption that Mrs. Case WAS the stalker he had seen multiple times. To Rome, it made total sense that she was watching him. In fact, she had previously told him to his face that she would be. Rome did not believe in coincidences. Not since he had witnessed the secret struggle between good and evil going on all around him. It had to be her! The real question was what she wanted with the boys.

As the fearless four approached the door to Mrs. Case's room, the air felt thicker. There was an almost tangible energy permeating from the room and wafting down the hallway. Rome looked at the space between the door and the floor and saw flashes of multi-colored lights flaunting recklessly inside the chamber. Strange, droning sounds echoed from the room also. Something peculiar was definitely going on in there.

Julian, being one who never backed down from a challenge, banged hard on the door three times and yelled for Mrs. Case. The strange sounds and lights stopped abruptly. Footsteps could be heard coming towards the door, but they stopped when they neared the exit. For a few seconds, there was no sound or movement. Then, Rome's dragon ears could hear the slightest whispering, but he could not make out the words.

Eventually, the door opened revealing Mrs. Case alone in her room. At first glance, nothing appeared out of the ordinary. The group waited patiently until Mrs. Case spoke.

"Oh, Rome and Julian," she said. "What can I do for you boys? And who are your friends?"

Camela spoke up. "Aye, madam. My name is Camela Rider and this is my consigliere, Krysta Valanche. You must be Principal Case. It is you whom I should blame for the atrocious and deplorable education my brother has been receiving in your public facility. I was not sure that it was possible, but he is actually more moronic now than when I left him last year. So, in actuality, I should be thanking you."

"Well, aren't you a saucy, little imp," said Mrs. Case. She patted Camela on the head. "I'll bet you harbor these ill feelings toward your brother because you feel your own inadequacy will be abundantly clear in your parents' eyes unless you constantly undermine him and show how much better you are than Julian. It must be hard living your life in permanent fear that you will let your parents down by not being perfect. That must be why you decided to rebel against the most important thing your parents taught you." She shifted her gaze towards Krysta. "She's the perfect vehicle for achieving your deception. The perfect collaborator to create a fall back plan if you were ever to let your parents down. So childish."

Camela backed up slightly. "You are perceptive, indeed." She said. "It's almost as if you have sight beyond normal sight. That is quite an interesting trait to have for a simple school headmaster."

Mrs. Case laughed merrily. "I was a guidance counselor for many years, dear. And I happen to be very good at reading people's behaviors. So, what can I do for you all?"

"We were hoping to talk to you about a certain necklace you may have," said Rome.

"Well," said Mrs. Case. "The only necklace I ever wear is this one." She reached into her shirt and pulled out an orb about the size of a golf ball attached to a leather cord around her neck. The color was such a dark red that it almost looked black. There were three or four rings encircling it like the planet Saturn. She held it out from her neck for the kids to see. "My parents left me this in a safe deposit box back home about ten years ago. They said it was my birthright, but I just thought it was a family heirloom. It was not until recently that I began to see exactly what its uses were." She smiled darkly. "Do you guys want to see what it can do?"

Before she received an answer, she let go of the orb, but it did not succumb to gravity. Instead, it came to life hovering right in front of Mrs. Case's eyes and glowing eerily. Streaks of purple and red swirled in and out of each other inside the sphere, and the rings started to rotate around the exterior.

As they spun faster, an audible whistling began to emit from the necklace. At last the orb flashed a brilliant light and sent a shockwave directly at the foursome. All of them flew back into the hallway and slumped against the walls.

Rome looked up to see Mrs. Case suspended in the air with her arms raised up to the ceiling. She caught Rome's gaze and smiled wickedly at him. From somewhere inside her chest, long, black fingers stretched out towards the orb. They extended until an entire, ghostly arm appeared from within Mrs. Case's torso. The hand portion moved to underneath the frenzied orb and shut tightly on it. Mrs. Case drifted slowly towards Rome staring intently at him. Rome could see that her irises had lost most of their color and the majority of her sclera was stained black. There was wind churning all around her and causing her hair to blow wildly like some kind of banshee.

Now right on top of Rome, she spoke in an otherworldly voice that echoed on itself. "You cannot stop me Rome Lockheed. Nor can any of your companions. I am beyond defeat inside this shell. Not even a dragon from Volcana stands a chance against me. You shall perish in this hallway along with your merry band of buffoons."

The dark spectral hand that extended from her body tapped its fingers on the side of Rome's face. Then, it reared back as if to strike him down, and she threatened him again. "My Master will invade this realm soon enough. All that is green and blue will fall into complete oblivion!"

Rome blinked his eyes and let loose an eye aura attack on Mrs. Case. The flames caught the mystical hand causing it to retract as if wounded. Mrs. Case recoiled in pain as Rome stood up to face her. He fired another round of eye flames right at Mrs. Case's body which knocked her far back into the dorm room. He grabbed Julian's arm and pulled him to his feet. Krysta had already picked Camela up and slung her over her shoulder. The three of them took off down the hall as if they were running for their lives.

"I think it is safe to say, she is NOT just a principal of a small town school!" shouted Rome.

"Dude! Dude, dude, dude, dude!!! What was that hand coming out of her??!!" screamed Julian. "Mr. Jones never mentioned anything about that in our training!"

"Duck," yelled Krysta.

Riders of Fire and Ice

The three of them fell to the ground just before a hovering Mrs. Case slammed into them. She flew directly over their backs and slowed to a stop at the end of the hallway. She pivoted around to face them and landed softly on the ground. The orb still floated in front of her with crazy colors emitting off the spinning rings.

Rome looked up from his prone position to analyze Mrs. Case more. The spiny, ghost fingers reemerged from her sternum and clasped the orb again. Then, Mrs. Case's face began to change. It started as only a black, hazy outline surrounding her head, but as she spoke, skeletal features flashed in and out of view. Her voice was a gurgled mess of raspy echoes clearly audible over the sounds of the torrent winds surrounding her.

"Fire dragon!" she hissed. "You are lost in this war. I will rip you and your fleshling to pieces! As for you, ice serpent. I shall avenge my fallen comrade by playing in your blood by sunset!"

Mrs. Case began to float again and cackle maniacally. The wraithlike arm let go of the orb and moved to extend form her left shoulder. At the same time, another arm extended from her right shoulder and pointed at the group.

"You are but vermin trapped on a sinking ship," snarled Mrs. Case. "I will rip you apart for my Master!"

The four kids could not move. They were completely petrified in that hallway. None of them could actually comprehend what they were witnessing. It was like something out of a horror movie, and it was absolutely terrifying to behold. It was the thing nightmares were made of.

Just then, Cecilia Parker stuck her head out of one of the rooms between the heroes and Mrs. Case. She looked at Rome and the others then looked at Mrs. Case and let out a shriek.

Before Rome could even move a muscle, Mrs. Case grabbed Cecilia around her mouth and waist and flew away. She rounded the corner and rocketed down the hallway towards the front door riding an invisible wind current. Rome and the others collected themselves, then ran after Mrs. Case.

To save his breath, Rome began communication on the spatial linking with Julian.

"Where do you think she is going?"

"No idea, dude. We need to catch her

before she does anything to Cecilia. You think you could pick up her scent with your dragon nose?"

"Absolutely. We need to find a good place to change and pursue her."

Krysta jumped in on the boys' conversation. "We must be wary, vigilant, and cautious while tracking her. I feel that this is not an ordinary adversary. Also, she has claimed a hostage. That leaves us little room for error, mistake, or miscalculation."

Rome and the others headed straight for the exit in the front of the dormitories. Once there, they ran outside into the rain. They were in luck as a downpour had forced almost everyone inside. The weather was good for getting rid of witnesses, but it also left Rome soggy and wet. If they had to fight, the elements would surely be against him.

The group ran to the side of the building by a large dumpster and storage space. Krysta put Camela back on her feet and analyzed her for injuries. Once satisfied that Camela was not hurt, Krysta stood next to Rome and waited for The Great Synergy to happen. Julian rolled his die.

In a flash, the two dragons appeared, and the Rider siblings transformed into their knightly gear. Julian climbed on to Rome carefully avoiding his spinal spikes. Krysta lowered her head so Camela could do her patented slide down her neck. They were ready for battle should it come down to it.

Both dragons flapped their mighty wings, and soon enough, the entire party was airborne. They were careful to avoid any bystanders who might espy them accidentally. The dragons climbed high in the sky and took off directly east in pursuit of the villain.

Rome used his dragon nose to locate Mrs. Case's scent. He found it almost immediately. It was a foul odor. It was one that he would never forget. He also picked up on Cecelia's scent. Her usual clover-like smell was almost completely overtaken by the stench from Mrs. Case What was she?"

"Any luck finding that crazed lunatic, dragon?" yelled Julian.

Rome glanced over to Krysta to make sure she was tracking Mrs. Case as well. Apparently both dragons were hunting down this enemy with remarkable precision. They flew lower barely missing the treetops while picking up formidable speed. Rome knew exactly where they were headed. Back to the lake in the woods. But why? Was Mrs. Case making a last stand against them? If so, would they be able to defeat her? What exactly WAS she?

The dragons flew increasingly low since they were far away from civilization. They needed a visual confirmation of their prey in order to attempt an attack. She was moving fast. Even faster than when Rome had tried to chase her in the woods. Obviously, wind currents were stronger outside making her nigh uncatchable.

"There's the witch!" called Camela. "She makes haste on our starboard side!"

Sure enough, Mrs. Case's bright red orb was easily seen weaving in and out of trees in the forest below them. Fujin's Teardrop was her escape, but also her betrayal. Her trajectory had her heading undeviatingly toward the lake shore where the boys had encountered the Hydrotaur the previous evening. The party watched from above as she hovered into the clearing and stopped at the lake's edge. Both dragons landed between Mrs. Case and the wood line with the idea that she would be backed against an unnavigable body of water. She turned around to face her pursuers and cast Cecilia's unconscious body to the ground.

The knights jumped off their dragons prepared for any attack Mrs. Case might throw at them. Julian quickly rolled his die, and Artemis materialized in his hands. He drew back a silver arrow with its picturesque green plumage and aimed it right between Mrs. Case's eyes. Camela readied the Frostshard as the two dragons fell into defensive positions on either side of the Rider children. The rain had stopped.

"Let her go!" roared Rome. "Or you will suffer unending agony!"

"Tsk, tsk, tsk silly serpent," she replied while waving a finger at him. "Your flames cannot hurt me." Her eyes went completely dark. "But if you so desire to destroy this body, I welcome your inferno." Again, the two skeletal, black arms came out of her shoulders, and her face flashed a skull-like quality. An aura of black energy surrounded Mrs. Case as she stared intently at the party.

"What sorcery is this?" asked Julian.

"It matters not, knight," sneered Rome.

"She has invited my firestorm, and I will see her burn!"

Rome leapt at the frightening faculty member who dodged to the left of the shore. Now, with Rome in between Mrs. Case and Cecilia, he unleashed a blazing fire stream. After a few seconds, Rome stopped and looked for any remains. To his surprise, instead he saw Mrs. Case floating twenty feet above the ground completely unscathed.

Mrs. Case cackled down at him. "You will see me burn, you say? What a bunch of hot air! I will shred you into ribbons."

The black aura that surrounded Mrs. Case began reforming. It became a three dimensional sphere vibrating in one of Mrs. Case's extra hands. In the blink of an eye, the sphere came shooting from Mrs. Case and crashed into Rome's shoulder. There was a mild explosion which caused Rome to retreat slightly. When he tried to retaliate with a fire attack, Rome realized he could not move. The black aura that had surrounded Mrs. Case now encapsulated Rome. Some dark magic was at work here. It must have paralyzed him somehow, and now, Rome was an easy target.

Just as this thought rattled around in Rome's head, Mrs. Case swooped down towards him. The dead, black fingers morphed into crescent blades like the scythe found on the Grim Reaper's sickle. Unable to defend himself, Rome fell under her lethal attack. Mrs. Case pummeled him with slashes and hacks while she crowed in hysteria. Sparks flew from where the ethereal blades connected with Rome's scales. Could his armor hold up?

Mrs. Case continued her relentless assault until one of her weaponized arms froze in mid strike. Then, the other arm turned to ice right before her eyes. From her right came one of Krysta's tremendous claws sending Mrs. Case tumbling into the shallows of the lake. She looked up from the mud and reached out her human hand. The black aura that had immobilized Rome flew from his body back to Mrs. Case's where it encircled her again. She stood up and inspected her icy appendages.

"An interesting technique," she grunted at Krysta who flew over to stand next to Rome. "But you only delay the inevitable." Mrs. Case closed her eyes and twisted her head slightly. All of a sudden, both of her frozen arms shattered into shards like crushed ice from a freezer and fell feebly all around her. A second later, they both sprouted again from her shoulders and materialized completely restored. "This beach will run crimson with dragon blood!"

Rome and Krysta exchanged looks of concern.

Chapter Fifteen

Mrs. Case's face was now almost entirely transformed into a macabre, black skull. The dark energy aura pulsed rhythmically in tandem with her breath. Facing the group, she raised her bladed arms into an attack position, and she spoke in her demonic voice.

"Humans and dragons relying on hope to defend their realm. So pitiful to watch. This world is destined to fall back into darkness as it was in the beginning. An eternal nightfall of agony wrought by the Earth's original monarch. The Tyrant King will return to his throne, and he will rule this planet through fear and merciless war mongering. His armies will soon blanket these lands, BUT you shall be the first victims of my wraith-blades." One of the weapons came close to Mrs. Case's face. A serpentine, forked tongue slithered out and licked the pulsating blade. "They long to feast on dragon flesh again. They long to..."

Before she could finish, a streaking, silver

arrow shot passed Rome's head straight towards Mrs. Case. She barely flinched as she caught the arrow in her hand merely inches from her chest with reflexes beyond any Rome had ever seen.

"That's enough of your verbal diarrhea," said Julian. "We are the defenders of this realm. You will die, demoness!"

Mrs. Case held the arrow to her face and sniffed it. "Arrows of the Gods? How interesting." She snapped the arrow in half. "Do you possess the Die of Hope? Mankind's last, dire attempt to repel their overwhelming annihilation. A pathetic girl's blunder shrouded by hysterically feeble hope; the weakest and most worthless emotion exhibited by Earth's vermin. My Master will be thoroughly pleased when I pry it from your dead fingers!"

"Enough, enchantress!" yelled Camela. She pointed a fine finger at her and sneered. "We are four warriors strong. We are bound by The Great Synergy. You will not depart this beach alive!"

"For Camelot!" shouted Julian.

He fired two arrows directly at Mrs. Case who pivoted to dodge them. Rome lunged at her and launched a flurry of strikes. Like two battling swordsmen, Rome and Mrs. Case exchanged swings and blocks creating hundreds of miniature explosions every time claw clashed with blade. Rome finally missed wildly with one attack which allowed Mrs. .Case to sidestep and land two quick spinning strikes on Rome's side. As he turned around to lumber toward her, Mrs. Case hit him with a wind blast which knocked him down the beach.

At that moment, Krysta landed behind Mrs. Case and snapped her teeth at the hovering demon. Mrs. Case shoved her black arms into Krysta's mouth holding it open. Krysta reared back her forearm and swung it at Mrs. Case's torso. Riding the air currents, Mrs. Case flipped sideways to avoid the attack. She completed an aerial cartwheel which forced Krysta's head sideways and flipped the ice dragon onto her back with a thud. Mrs. Case's orb let loose another wind blast which sent Krysta sliding and twisting into the shallows.

Mrs. Case lowered her blades to her side and slowly stalked towards Krysta's motionless body. As she approached, however, clouds began to form around her head. In seconds, an entire snowstorm swirled distractingly in front of her face. It caused her to shield her eyes with her human arms and stop her approach a few seconds.

Mrs. Case whirled around to see Camela hindering her with the use of The Frostshard. Her ghastly mouth let out a wicked hiss and she lunged at Camela with her black blades ready to slash. She landed multiple blows on Camela's armor which forced Camela to stop her spell and defend herself with her scepter. This was to little avail as Camela was hardly a match for Mrs. Case's onslaught. She defended herself admirably, but Mrs. Case's attacks were too fast and too fierce. Fujin's Teardrop glowed brightly as a torrent of wind launched Camela's weakened body onto her butt nearly twenty feet away. Camela quickly hobbled to her feet and dashed for cover.

Julian took the brief pause as an opportunity to attack with his newly materialized weapon, Odin's Gungnir. He charged Mrs. Case from the side, but somehow, she must have sensed his attack, because she was able to move at the last second. Julian did not miss completely though, as the tip of Gungnir tore through part of Mrs. Case's blouse. Julian pulled back Gungnir and swung the back end of his weapon at her head. She blocked it with one of her arms and rode the air back a few feet to recover herself. With her human hand, she touched where the tear had occurred. To Julian's amazement, her hand was tarnished red with blood, and Mrs. Case chuckled softly.

"She CAN bleed!" shouted Julian.

Mrs. Case fumed at Julian. "Foolish fleshling! You know nothing of the danger you confront. My host can bleed, this is true. But I am eternal. I am dark energy." The ebony tongue emerged from her skull and licked the blood from her fingers. "How I have missed that taste! Bring me more!"

Julian repositioned his feet and threw Gungnir as hard as he could at Mrs. Case like an Olympic javelinist. One of her black arms swatted the spear out of the air. She came at Julian and pinned him to the ground. Her ophidian tongue lashed wildly throwing saliva all around. The other bladed appendage reared back as if to come down like a guillotine, but before she could land the deadly blow, Gungnir came hurdling back to its master. It flew pointed end first into Mrs. Case's ghost hand stabbing it into the ground.

Mrs. Case shrieked, which allowed Julian to escape her clutches. He ran to where Camela had hidden herself and Cecilia behind a pile of logs.

Both Rider children used their Talismans' abilities to stop their gnarly nemesis, but they only succeeded in slowing her down; and angering her.

Mrs. Case pulled on Gungnir until it finally came unstuck from the ground. She whirled around to find her opponent, but found only Rome gliding down at her and kicking her in her sternum. He followed up by swinging his massive claws at Mrs. Case, but she was able to fend off his attacks with her dark appendages and Gungnir. The two danced in battle until Mrs. Case trapped the haft of Gungnir behind Rome's head and twisted him down to the ground. As Mrs. Case lowered her blades for a kill shot, Rome grabbed them with his claws leaving the two in a stalemate.

Mrs. Case moved her skeleton head close to Rome. While the two struggled to gain an advantage, she screeched in his ear. "Your resistance is futile, lizard. I will see you split wide open." Her tongue went to lick Rome's face, but he strained to pull away from its touch.

"You will be fed to flames, hag!" rumbled Rome.

Just then, Krysta hit Mrs. Case in the back with an ice blast. The force sent her flying over

Rome back into the murky water. Rome got up from the ground and shook his head. Krysta stood next to him as the two watched Mrs. Case hover above the water. Julian ran in between the two dragons as Gungnir whistled back into his hands.

Mrs. Case shot up from the water high into the air with her necklaced orb lighting up dramatically and acting as a tracking device for the heroes below. Just before she got out of eyesight, she came soaring back down at an incredible rate of speed. Rome opened his mouth and shot fire at her. Krysta did the same with her ice breath, but Mrs. Case adeptly dodged the attacks on her way towards the threesome. She swooped down on the party and kicked Julian in the chest. As she flew up again, she manipulated her aura and flashed her wraith-blades almost in slow motion. She crested the height of her retreat and began another descent with remarkable alacrity.

Again, the dragons discharged their elemental blasts at her, but she could not be hit. Upon reaching the duo, she hooked both wraith-blades on Rome's head spikes and pulled him to the ground like a rodeo bull. She immediately hovered up a few feet and detonated another wind blast at Rome's chest which launched him all the way back to the tree line. In the same motion, she spun her blades around slashing Krysta across her face. Krysta brought her wings over her shoulders at her assailant, but Mrs. Case jumped back avoiding the diamond-like scales.

Krysta changed her strategy and turned her body so she could attack with her tail spike. Mrs. Case defended herself with her blades proficiently until the power of The Frostshard tipped the odds in Krysta's favor. As Mrs. Case was hindered by another miniature, blinding snowstorm, Krysta landed several blows on Mrs. Case's left shoulder and right forearm.

Mrs. Case, realizing she was losing the battle, flew back from the blizzard stepping into the lake shallows. From there, she ignited another of Fujin's Teardrop wind blasts at Krysta who protected herself with her wings. With separation gained, Mrs. Case located where Camela was remotely antagonizing her and threw a couple of smaller, purple wind balls at her. Camela dove away just before the projectiles exploded the ground at her feet into an eruption of sand and random, wooded beach debris. Krysta, concerned for her sister's life, quickly used her ice breath to freeze the water around Mrs. Case's ankles.

As Mrs. Case struggled to break free from the ice, Julian rushed at her with Gungnir in a jousting stance. He dug the spear tip into the dirt and propelled himself up into the air. While airborne, he rolled his die into his empty palm causing Pridwen to appear on his arm. He pulled his legs into his chest and positioned the gilded shield in front of his knees. To finish off the maneuver, Julian cannonballed right into Mrs. Case knocking her to the ground and shattering the ice at her feet.

After the collision, Julian skidded across the lakeshore water riding Pridwen like a skim board. Once far enough away, he did a backflip off the shield, landed acrobatically, and dropped his magical die into the mud by his side. Artemis appeared in Julian's waiting hands, shining in the lake reflection.

"Smile she-witch!" whispered Julian as he let a green-plumed arrow fly.

Mrs. Case stood and spun around just in time for Artemis's arrow to pierce her in her shoulder. She jerked back and fell to her knees. Julian notched another arrow and aimed between her eyes. Before he could take the shot, Mrs. Case threw her head back and squealed. Her black aura changed formations eventually resolving itself into that paralyzing sphere in her hand. It shot from her hand at light speed and connected with Julian causing him to drop Artemis and fall down stunned. The aura enveloped and immobilized him on the ground like he was caught in some kind of electric Taser field.

Krysta ran at Mrs. Case's side and attempted to smack her with her wing, but Mrs. Case was able to block the attack with her bladed arms. However, the force of Krysta's wings pushed Mrs. Case back away from the water. Realizing an opportunity, Krysta quickly unloaded another ice blast from her mouth at Mrs. Case. At the same time, Mrs. Case released an air attack at Krysta. The two elemental bursts collided which caused a tremendous eruption and a discordant thunder across the countryside.

The outburst slammed Krysta back into the water. She tried to stand, but collapsed in the shallows and closed her eyes apparently lacking the energy required to continue fighting. Mrs. Case, on the other hand, had avoided much of the combustion by riding the air currents out of harm's way. Her clothes were tattered and the limbs on her left side appeared to have suffered multiple bruises and cuts.

She hovered briefly, assessing the situation beneath her. Julian was still stuck in her black-aura incarceration, and Krysta lay immobile in the lake shoals. Mrs. Case finally took notice of Artemis's arrow lodged in her shoulder. She grotesquely wrenched it from its spot with her teeth and spat it into the water below showing her superhuman threshold for pain. Next, she calmly alit on the ground and began stalking towards Krysta. Over her head, her wraith blades scraped against each other causing cascading sparks to fall around her and fizzle out as they hit the lake water.

"And now you shall perish, wretched reptile," scowled Mrs. Case as she twirled her bifurcated, slathering tongue around the crimson pool of blood collected on her shoulder. "Prepare to join your ancestors in extinction."

Chapter Sixteen

Rome had finally pulled himself together enough to attempt an assault on the injured Mrs. Case. He galloped towards her with his head down in a battering ram position. The allies were losing this battle, and Rome realized he needed to change the tide using extreme measures. Or maybe he was just getting angrier like the ire in his belly.

Mrs. Case turned at the last second and caught Rome's head in her human hands. Rome's momentum drove her towards the edge of the forest though she pushed back ferociously. She began stabbing wildly at Rome's back and shoulders with her wraith-blades, but the fire dragon's scales deflected most of the damage. Rome whipped his tail around one of Mrs. Case's legs and pulled as hard as he could.

Mrs. Case must have realized that Rome was about to rip her leg out of socket because she quickly countered with another wind blast from

Fujin's Teardrop directly under Rome's neck. This forced a choking Rome to relinquish his tail grip and disengage from the shoving match. On his retreat, however, he swatted one of his mighty wings skyward which sent Mrs. Case flying above the trees.

She regained her balance in the air and elevated her bladed appendages angrily. She spit blood from her mouth which diluted into the lake water in tight, red ripples. It was evident that she was no longer pleased with the injuries she sustained. She neck twitched as she spoke to Rome in her otherworldly rasp.

"What do you hope to accomplish, drake?" she spewed. Her human hand motioned to the battlefield below her. "Your allies are incapacitated. Your energy level plummets by the second. You are but one solitary salamander in way over your head." She crossed her arms as if relishing the next line. "I have slaughtered dozens of your kind during battles long forgotten to the history of this world. You stand no chance against me."

"And just who are you, mighty dragon slayer?" mocked Rome. "You are certainly not a human school headmaster. Are you more sewage that has accidentally seeped its way out of The Void?"

"I'll tell you who that is," came a voice from inside the woods. Much to Rome's surprise, Mr. Jones came strolling through the trees and stood next to him. He reached up to pat Rome's chest. Humans always enjoyed physical contact to reinforce feelings. This was a foreign concept to dragons.

"It does me good to see you, Young Master," said Mr. Jones. "I must say I am very impressed with your battle prowess thus far. You and your new friends have performed sensationally against this formidable foe, but I think I can be of some valuable assistance from here on out."

"Who is this cockroach crawling before me," sneered Mrs. Case from above the trees. "Another skin-walker to add to the massacre? Come closer, human, and I'll flay you wide open! You will feel the sting of my wraith-blades."

"It's funny that you mention those demonic devices," laughed Mr. Jones. "You see, I am not your average 'skin-walker'. I know things that most humans here do not. For instance, I know that you are obviously not the true Mrs. Case. I know that you are, in fact, a Nocturn that has possessed said lady." Mr. Jones smiled widely. "And I've come to take her back."

The presence inside Mrs. Case let out the most gruesome laugh Rome had ever heard. She hacked and coughed in between deep cackles while lashing around her freakish tongue A Nocturn? Of course! Why hadn't Rome thought of that? Julian said they were the things of nightmares, but he admitted he had never seen one. So, this is what they looked like. Kind of? He switched his gaze from Mr. Jones back to the hovering Mrs. Case.

"You cannot have this husk unless you pull me from it!" she gargled.

"Then, that is what I shall do," replied Mr. Jones. "You see, demon, I know that ALL Nocturns have individual weaknesses." He began pacing back and forth in full lecture mode. "These inherent weaknesses, or inadequacies are never the same for each one, like human fingerprints or snowflakes." He paused and tapped his fingertips together to accentuate his words. Then, proceeded striding confidently back and forth while Mrs. Case eyed him warily.

"Some of the oldest Nocturns have been

documented and studied regularly over the centuries. Since the average person can easily be possessed by Nocturns, mankind came up with a way to distinguish between the different ones. This identification allowed mankind to expunge them with as little harm to the host as possible. Under the good King Arthur's watch, researchers began detailing as many cases as they could of these "possessions". They kept a precise record of the characteristics of each instance. Soon, they began seeing patterns in the behaviors of some of these ancient beings. Along with the help of dragons, humans began perfecting exorcisms and created a registry of outcomes. With this information, they were able to differentiate between the Nocturns and come to know them by nickname or moniker directly associated with each Nocturn's weakness. I happen to be in ownership of that catalogue." He leaned towards the hovering Mrs. Case. "In other words, I know your name, devil!"

Mrs. Case laughed morbidly. "What good will that do you, mage? I am eternal! I am ethereal! I am dark energy, and I'll carve you up right after that overgrown alligator!"

She suddenly flew at the duo with urgency

and mania. Rome took a defensive stance and braced for impact. Mr. Jones, conversely did not move a muscle. In fact, he pushed his glasses back up on his nose and smiled at the attacking banshee.

"You will do nothing of the sort, Nameless" shouted Mr. Jones emphatically. "I will call you out by your name, and then cast you back to the trenches of The Void!"

Mrs. Case came to a screeching halt a few feet from the heroes. She hung in the air lifelessly for about five seconds. Then, she opened her eyes to reveal the pitch-black sclera of the Nocturn inside. She began to shake violently, and her extremities flailed in all directions. At the same time, a very low, strange shrieking began to emit from her body (not her mouth).

Mr. Jones took another step towards her. "You are the Nameless, aren't you?" He looked at Rome. "This Nocturn's weakness is its surname. Once we know its name, it will be diminished enough for us to expel it from Mrs. Case." Mr. Jones chuckled at his accidental, scholastic pun.

Mrs. Case stopped jolting and touched down on the ground. Her ebony eyes were sharply focused on Mr. Jones, and the low shriek evolved to a sound like the caterwauling of a malcontent tomcat.

"The power of the light will pull you from this host, ancient one," said Mr. Jones calmly. "I will have you removed by your title!" Mr. Jones stood back and steadied himself. "Zaghnal, The Wraith-sickle! Leave this body!"

Mrs. Case's head flung back, and her throat let go an earsplitting scream. After a few deafening seconds, her body fell like hot spaghetti noodles to the ground. Mr. Jones hurried over to her and began checking her vitals. He leaned her up against a bush so she would not asphyxiate and pulled his glasses off so they would not impede his examination.

"She's breathing, and I have a pulse!" cried Mr. Jones brightly.

Rome did not have time to celebrate as something caught his attention in the woods. Rome assumed he was locked eye to eye with the Nocturn that had recently exited Mrs. Case's body. It stared at Rome through lifeless, angry eye sockets. From what Rome could see, it had the upper body and head of a skeleton, but no lower appendages appeared below where its waist should be. Instead, the ribcage faded into nothingness at ground level making it look like it was floating. When it realized Rome saw it, it rattled its jaw at him and hauled tail further into the woods.

"Wizard," called Rome. "That thing is making a break for it!"

"See to your fallen comrades, Rome," said Mr. Jones. "Leave the Nocturn to me."

Mr. Jones took off into the woods hoping to track the weakened Nocturn while Rome surveyed the carnage. As Camela skittishly popped out from her hiding place, Rome started towards Julian who was now free from Zaghnal's prison. He was limping and clearly out of breath. Rome and Julian had been beaten soundly, but they knew they had to harness whatever energy they had left and surge on.

"Rome!" called Camela. "Is Krysta okay?" There was panic in Camela's voice as she was clearly shaken and concerned for her fallen sister. That's when Rome noticed that Camela appeared seriously injured so much so that she hobbled on one foot and cradled her left arm against her chest.

It was evident that The Great Synergy affected both parties whether it was done properly or simulated.

"Jules, the girls need help," Rome sent across the spatial linking.

"No problem, dude. I'll roll out my number six," returned Julian with a decent amount of giddiness.

"Do whatever you have to do. I need to follow Mr. Jones. He will need my assistance."

"Alright, dude. Just gimme a second."

Julian ran to Camela who had stumbled to her knees trying to get to Krysta. Julian rolled his die, and it landed with the six pips facing the siblings. Julian instantly held in his hand a wrought-iron version of the well-known symbol, The Caduceus, identical to the one on hospital signs. Julian rotated the trinket in his hand curiously inspecting all sides of the mysterious object. Much to Julian's surprise, this summoning was not artistically decorated or overly lavish in any way. The intertwining serpents lacked eye-catching color or any kind of sumptuous ornamentation, and Hermes's wings on the top even looked a tad rusted. Julian wondered what he was to do with something so mediocre.

There was a flash of light from the emblem, and Camela was enveloped in a green, glittering circle of sparkles. The bruises and scrapes on her exposed skin remarkably disappeared. The dents and dings on her armor reformed leaving it looking brand new as well. Even her disheveled pigtails were restored to their trademark quirkiness. When the green twinkles faded away, Camela stood up fully cured and noticeably amazed.

"It may not look like much, but this is one of the greatest additions to my arsenal," said Julian with his patented smirk. "The Caduceus can heal all your wounds inflicted by the Darkbrands in battle. And thanks to The Great Synergy..."

Krysta bounded up to the Rider children completely refreshed and full of vigor. The representative from Iglacia coiled her neck around Camela in a show of affection between the two sisters. Once she let go, she stared at Camela for a few seconds until the Valkyrie armor-clad girl sighed and shirked her shoulders angrily.

"Fine!" she exclaimed as she swiveled to face her brother. "Krysta claims it is necessary that

I show you my gratitude for your assistance just now. Apparently, I am indebted to you for this noble deed." She crossed her petite arms and frowned. "I am only in wonderment as to what took you so long. Did you wish for me to perish on this battlefield? Of all the brainless, incorrigible mistakes one could...."

Krysta nudged her with her white head, interrupting her.

"What?" cried Camela. "Is he not brainless? Very well." She looked at Julian and pouted. "You fought bravely today, brother. You embodied the valor and the courage of The House of Rider greatly."

"That's what I'm talkin' about!" yelled Julian. "Woohoo! Yeah, baby!" Julian jumped around and rode an imaginary horse in a circle hooting. "Gimme some scale, Krysta!" Julian extended his hand in a high five position towards the dragon, but she rebuffed his proposal .

"That's enough, you simpleton!" fumed Camela. "While you dance around like a buffoon, your dragon has left you!"

In fact, Rome had disappeared from sight

entirely. Julian was panicked for a split second. Had Rome run after Mr. Jones on his own? He remembered when Rome had foolishly rushed into the woods back when the boys began training. Rome had blindly charged into the unknown desperately looking for Julian without knowing what dangers lay before him. Dragons seemed rather reckless to Julian; and loyal to the point of endangerment. What extravagant extremes they possessed thought Julian as he opened up the spatial linking again.

"Yo, Rome! Where'd ya go, man?" he said as calmly as he could.

"I am following Mr. Jones's scent. I will not allow our leader to fight this thing on his own. I am bleeding under my left eye, so to join us, simply follow the trail of blood on the leaves I brushed by."

Julian suddenly realized he had not even attended to his own wounds. He ran his finger under his left eye, and laughed to himself when he saw the red liquid painted on it. Who knew what perilous evil they were about to face. Julian knew they needed to be prepared, so he decided to use The Caduceus on himself/Rome as soon as he could track down his brother.

"Ice dragon, come with me," Julian ordered. "Camela, stay here and attend to Mrs. Case and Cecilia. We will have to figure them out later."

Julian looked to the tree line. He noticed a few broken tree limbs near the edge. He figured that was as good as any place to start so he galloped over to them and observed a few specks of blood on the leaves. Then, with the careless abandon of a dragon, he took off into the woods.

Chapter Seventeen

Rome pushed through the trees trampling and destroying most of the local flora. He paused briefly multiple times to make sure he was following the right scents. He could not smell Mr. Jones, but it didn't really matter. The rotten smell of The Void was so pungent in Rome's nostrils that it made him nauseous. He followed it with ease yet cautious trepidation.

Finally, Rome came to a skidding halt as he entered an ample clearing. In the center stood a large tree that created a canopy of large, green leaves overhead. Zaghnal, The Wraith-sickle lingered underneath the tree facing off against Rome's mentor. The Nocturn appeared much more besieged than when the party had first encountered it. Its blades drooped down by its side, and it appeared to hunch over as if laboring to breathe.

Mr. Jones spoke overtly to Rome without

taking his eyes off the shade. "It is beleaguered, but not yet defeated. It has come here to try to gather more energy from The Void to sustain its existence on our plane."

"I do not understand," said Rome. "We are in the middle of the woods. Where would it be drawing energy from?"

"By Dracula's fangs!" shouted Mr. Jones. "How silly of me! I forgot you cannot see what I see through my glasses." He moved closer to Rome. "There is a portal on this tree, Young Master. It is operational, as well. We have two clear objectives here; eliminate Nameless and eliminate the portal."

Rome remembered Mr. Jones's glasses were able to detect portals and see into The Void. These specially crafted lenses were handed down to him from his predecessor, Mr. Smith. Rome had looked into The Void one time a few months ago under careful supervision. There were truly dark and evil things crawling around in there constantly trying to get through to Earth. It had shaken him to his foundation to witness the abominations, but that was before he knew how powerful he would become. And now, he needed to hone those skills and destroy this Nocturn before it could cause any more trouble or threaten anyone else close to him.

This little tidbit of information also helped Rome understand something else that transpired recently. When the boys had faced off against the Hydrotaur, there was some gaseous, dark energy that shot through the trees and mended the Minotaur's detached horn. Apparently, all manner of wounded Darkbrands could summon dark energy from an open portal to remedy their deteriorating status. Great!

"We will need a great sacrifice to close the portal," continued Mr. Jones. "I have a plan though. Once the Nocturns are debilitated, they can easily be beaten. At this point, a robust, elemental attack should be enough to banish Zaghnal back to The Void. How is your energy supply? Do you have enough reserve in the tank?"

Rome smiled a toothy grin. "I have plenty of spirit left, sir. I will burn this fiend into nothingness."

"I can appreciate your fervor, Young Master," said Mr. Jones. "But I must warn you that the Nocturns are one of the oldest residents of this realm, and they should never be taken lightly. There is a REASON they have existed since the early days of this planet. They are as wily and persistent as they are ancient and evil. Exercise caution."

Taking Mr. Jones's advice, Rome moved himself precariously within striking range of Zaghnal. He wanted to make sure he had a contained stream of dragon fire so as not to burn down the entire forest. His mission was to eradicate Zaghnal, but what good would it be if he harmed his own allies too?

Zaghnal began a raspy, exasperated breathing. The tree behind it began to give off an eerie glow as dark energy started pouring out the portal and attaching itself to the Nocturn. Zaghnal really was growing stronger by the second. In fact, its wraith-blades had already raised into an attacking stance. Rome had to do something quickly before the fiend returned to full strength, and the portal closed again.

Rome inhaled turning his chest scales into brimstones and went to envelope Zaghnal, but the shadow sidestepped the flames and rushed him in a full-on flanking attack. Before Rome could react, Zaghnal performed an aerial cartwheel flipping directly over Rome's back. It landed five or six slashing attacks in quick succession to Rome's spine and ribs. Rome winced in pain as the demon landed and took off away from him.

Rome, who could not move as adeptly in this confined space, swiped his powerful tail at the retreating enemy. With skillful precision, Rome's tail struck Zaghnal sending it end over end and smashing into the portal tree. The collision bent the tree in half causing it to crash directly on top of Zaghnal.

The woods were still for a few seconds as a handful of rustling leaves fell silently to the ground. Rome stared at the wreckage intently. He could still feel the dark energy emitting from the tree and gathering around the Nocturn. His dragon senses noticed movement out of the corner of his eye, but he was too late in his reaction. Zaghnal's stunning energy orb shot out from behind the tree trunk and caught Rome on the snout. Once again, he was imprisoned in black, electric prison and unable to move.

Zaghnal approached the immobilized Rome with its tongue whipping around sadistically. It was almost upon him with its wraith-blades buzzing when Gungnir came whizzing over Rome's shoulder. It shot directly at Zaghnal's head and caught it on its chin. The force of Gungnir's impact took Zaghnal's lower jaw with it as it bolted into the fallen tree behind them.

The demon screamed in riotous pain that echoed throughout the woods and sent the remaining wildlife scurrying and flying for cover. Rome was immediately free of his restriction, but he was far more injured than he originally determined. He was sure to need The Caduceus's healing factor soon. Julian joined his dragon and stared at the Nocturn as it thrashed around the clearing.

Julian extended his arms out and mentally called for Gungnir to return to him. The majestic spear wiggled free from the tree trunk and started its flight back to Julian. Its trajectory led it impaling straight through Zaghnal's chest and into Julian's waiting hands.

"Zaghnal, The Wraith-sickle," said Julian. "You are hereby exiled back to the darkness to scavenge among the wretched." He walked over to where the demon struggled to stay upright. "You tell your master that we will not surrender our world to him. We will fight, and we will win!"

From somewhere inside the hollow skull, Zaghnal managed to speak. "Mortal. I'll seeeeeee you in eterrrrrrnal oooooblivion."

Julian pulled out Pandora's Die of Hope and tossed it in the air a couple times. Finally, he caught the die in his hand and dropped it onto the ground. In an instant, Gungnir disappeared from Julian's grip, and was replaced by a gigantic, pixelating sword. Julian took the massive blade in two hands and swung it over his shoulder as the remaining pixels drifted away.

The weight of the blade forced Julian to concentrate on maintaining his balance while it perched across his back. The sword itself looked to be over four feet long with the handle adding another foot to its length. The blade segment, obviously crafted by an absolute master, was forged from remarkable, pristine steel, and the hilt was fashioned from sturdy, tanned leather. At the end of the hilt was a golden sphere about the size of a cue ball. Two smaller yet similar versions sat aesthetically on both ends of the cross guard like silent sentries.   Twisting their way up the fuller of the sword about a foot were several thistle flowers fashioned from the same cinereal steel as the rest of the blade. The sheer sight of this weapon evoked both admiration and fright when one took into account the countless battles and bloodshed this legendary sword had witnessed. It was baronial yet haunting.

"Dragon," Julian spoke. "Let us light this fire."

Rome blinked a controllable amount of eye fire at Julian's magnificent sword, The Claymore. The flames danced around the sword like angry, fiery specters. The heat was so intense, that it made Julian's armor glow orange. He swiveled towards the agonizing Nocturn and proceeded with a downward strike right through the middle of its torso.

Zaghnal split into two halves that strobed in and out of sight. As quickly as Julian had made the cut, the demon fizzed out of view and joined the remaining dark energy flowing reversely into the portal. Mr. Jones ran over to the wicked tree and watched as the energy was sucked into the abyss.

Mr. Jones spoke as loud as he could over the mild torrent. "Today the universe witnesses the defeat of the Nocturn colloquially known as Nameless. Let it be known that this portal be purged of evil and sealed by the sacrifice of Zaghnal, The Wraith-sickle." He pulled a small flask from his back pocket and uncorked it. A familiar, blue mist flowed out of the bottle and surrounded the tree. As if driven by hundreds of tiny fireflies, the mist sparkled beautifully in the afternoon sun's rays which had caused the earlier rainclouds to move on.

The cacophony ended abruptly, and the woods were still again. Mr. Jones jumped off the fallen tree and made his way over to his young heroes. Krysta also weaved her way through the trees to join her allies in the clearing. She approached Mr. Jones cautiously while glancing at Rome a couple times for reassurance.

"Great gargoyles!" shouted Mr. Jones. "You must be Krysta Valanche from the Den of Iglacia. It is a tremendous honor to meet you, Master. I have never in all my years had the privilege of meeting a genuine ice dragon." Mr. Jones rubbed the back of his head slightly embarrassed. "Well, to be honest, I have only ever met ONE other dragon. But I digress. It is a pleasure to make your acquaintance." Mr. Jones bowed his head.

Krysta blinked her eyes a few times and bowed her head at Mr. Jones as well. She attempted to speak to the group. "Sharil ungatta moncrobin ver pas. Morgul klockte ver nan flora, cora, unt sacrin mora."

Mr. Jones stared blankly at her white face like he was reminiscing. "Draketongue is the most marvelous thing I've ever heard. I just wish I understood it." He bowed deeper this time. "Rome, if you would not mind translating?"

"The delegate from Iglacia says she is honored to meet you, Mr. Jones," said Rome. "She knows all about you and your dealings with Julian and myself. In not so many words, she said she's very impressed with your talents as a human."

Mr. Jones blushed slightly. "Thank you, Master. I am as equally rapt with your abilities. You and your Synergist Knight will make fine allies for us indeed."

Krysta exhaled some of her frozen breathe which hung in the air momentarily and eventually formed into a smiley face with a crooked icicle smile.

Julian interjected. "Mr. Jones! It is painfully obvious that you are obsessed with dragons. Seriously, you act like a seven-year old at a bounce house birthday party every time you meet one. Now, we have dire business to attend to here, and your little gushing episode is completely unnecessary."

"My apologies, Sir Julian," blushed Mr.

Jones. "You are quite right. Quite right, indeed."

"Crazy old coot," whispered Julian.

"Now, to the matters at hand," said Mr. Jones rubbing his hands together. "Sir Julian, if you would please start by healing yourself AND your dragon. Then, we will need to discuss the resolutions for the two damsels in distress back at the lake." Mr. Jones paused while The Caduceus's sparkly, green light encircled his two pupils. "I have many things to share with you all, and I hope to start immediately as I may run out of Transportation Incantation power at any minute."

As the emerald fluorescence diminished, and the warriors' wounds were mended, the group made its way back to the lakeshore to check on Lady Camela and the two "damsels". They had agreed that the dragon representatives should probably change back into their disguised forms in case Cecilia had come to her senses. It would probably be a little too much for her to take in at this juncture.

When the group finally arrived, Cecilia was still unconscious, but Mrs. Case was up and moving around. From what Rome could see, she appeared relatively unharmed. Even the wound at her shoulder was mysteriously mended. She was tending to Cecilia and talking to Camela. No doubt, Camela was giving her the full rundown of the events leading up to her exorcism. Rome wondered how long the woman had been under Zaghnal's spell. He hoped he would never be taken over by a Nocturn.

Camela saw the group coming through the trees and leapt to her feet. Due to The Great Synergy's dispelling, she was no longer clad in her Valkyrie armor, and she was back in her mundane school garb. She and her pigtails bounced up as the group approached and raced towards them emphatically. She ran right past her brother and embraced Krysta with a rigorous hug.

"Sister," she said. "I knew you were okay, but after a lengthy gap in communication, I began to fret for your safety. Mostly because of the company around you." She glared at Julian.

Julian was unfazed. "Sis, we've got some important news. This is Mr. Jones. His physical body is back in The United States, but he's been able to help us seal the portal in the woods and help us with our recovery. He's a friend who uses magic to transport people." Mr. Jones extended his hand to Camela and blinked a couple times.

"What need have we of this old man disguised as a hologram?" scoffed Camela. "I have found us our team's mage. Come, sister. You must meet the newest ally to join our cause." Camela led Krysta by the arm over to where Mrs. Case was watching over Cecilia.

"Charming lass," joked Mr. Jones. He wrapped the boys around their shoulders, and they followed the girls.

As they neared Mrs. Case, Rome took note of something. Mrs. Case held Cecilia in her arms, but she kept her left hand spread open about a foot away from Cecilia's face. There appeared to be a pixelating aura emitting from Mrs. Case's fingertips which swathed around the unconscious girl's head. He also took note of Mrs. Case's eyes. They were no longer her normal color, nor were they the deathly black of the Nocturn. Instead, there were kaleidoscopic rainbows undulating throughout the whites of her eyes. It was as if her pupils were surrounded by pulsating, psychedelic hues. Rome instinctively jumped at the woman and pushed her away.

"Get off her, demon!" he yelled. "Quick, Jules transform us! She is casting a curse on Cecilia!"

Rome braced himself for The Great Synergy's flash as he stood over Mrs. Case cowering on the ground. He was not sure exactly what was going on, but he knew he could not trust this woman anymore after she tried to kill him and his party.

"Relax, Rome," said Mrs. Case picking herself off the ground. "I am trying to help her." She walked towards him dusting sand off her dress, and he noticed her eyes were no longer a swirling medley of colors.

Mrs. Case continued in a rather sing-song voice. "She has been affected by the Nocturn's darkness. It's not quite a full-on possession, but she has undeniably fallen under the influence of Zhagnal the Wraith-sickle's darktouch. She will require light magic to wash away the curse that's overtaken her. I can provide that."

Rome was unsure and a little angry. He looked to his mentor. "Mr. Jones, what is she talking about? Is she telling the truth?"

Julian jumped in as well. "How do you know about Nocturns and Darkbrands?" he griped in an accusatory manner.

"Mr. Jones," cried Rome. "What exactly is going on here? Is this some kind of joke? Who is she?"

"It's okay, Young Master," soothed Mr. Jones. He placed his hands on his hips and nodded his head to Mrs. Case. "Perhaps, it's time you tell them who you really are, A.C. And, give them honesty. They deserve it."

Chapter Eighteen

Mrs. Case sighed and acknowledged her audience. "Boys, before I became a middle school principal, I was the student of a very wise and mysterious man. I spent about five years under his tutelage in my early twenties. He taught me about the impending war between Earth's residents and the Darkbrands. He also taught me what we mortals call 'magic'. You see, my parents gave me this before they died." She held out Fujin's Teardrop. "My teacher sought me out because of this heirloom. He told me about the power it contained, and how we would need it to defeat The Tyrant King. After five years, my teacher decided I was ready to explore the world and prepare for the inevitable invasion. He told me to seek out another former student of his who had taken up residence in Georgia." She looked at Mr. Jones. "I assume you are M.J.?"

"By the hairs of Hercules! Indeed, I am he!" exclaimed Mr. Jones. He walked up to Mrs. Case and shook her hand eagerly. "This truly is an amazing day. We have so much to catch up on. Your Talisman is quite powerful, indeed. I saw it in action from my hiding spot. So, Mr. Smith taught you the Dreamweaver spell, did he? He always told me I was not imaginative enough for that one. Please don't misunderstand me, he taught me some spectacular things, but he always said the Dreamweaver spell would need to be mastered by someone with a certain zest for life; a certain flair for the inventive; a kind of..."

"Hey, old man!" yelled Julian. "Can you stop your jabbering and tell us something useful? How can she help Cecilia?"

"Great hippogriff's hooves!" cried Mr. Jones. "Pardon my ramblings. Mrs. Case was inducing the Dreamweaver spell. The Dreamweaver spell was developed to help survivors of the Despot War deal with their nightmares from the battles they fought and the side effects from Darkbrand interaction. Almost like our modern-day PTSD but with an assortment of different maladies and madness. The spell allows the user to implement dreams of THEIR choosing into the distraught person's unconscious mind. The thinking was that solace could be found in a peaceful and pacific dreamscape. In this case, your classmate has been affected by the darktouch of a Nocturn which rendered her comatose. I am assuming that Mrs. Case intends to take the girl back to her dormitory and sedate her until tomorrow morning. With the Dreamweaver spell cast upon her, she will remember this whole experience as nothing more than whimsical, uplifting reveries."

"That was my intent," established Mrs. Case. "But I guess I should have consulted with those dearest to her first." She looked at Rome who was holding Cecilia from the torso up. "You must be her boyfriend. I am so sorry to have over-stepped my boundaries."

"Hey, old lady!" piped Camela. "Rome's not her boyfriend."

"That's right," chimed in Krysta. "Not yesterday, today, OR tomorrow!'

"Oh," said Mrs. Case taken aback. "Well, again, my apologies for the assumption. It's hard for me to keep up on my students' social lives. They seem to change daily." She addressed Rome as she came closer. "I always knew you were a special kid, Rome. From the first time you stepped off the bus at Dampier Middle School I knew you would make great things happen in this world. I had no idea what you would become. It's remarkable to know your true identity." She leaned down and began the spell on Cecilia again. Pixels sprinkled from her fingertips and her eyes resumed their colorful dance.

"Mr. Jones," pleaded Rome. "Is this for real? Is she another pupil of your teacher?"

"Why yes," agreed Mr. Jones moving closer to Rome and Cecilia. "Once I returned from my sabbatical of self-discovery, my teacher had already taken on another disciple and released her into the world. He told me about her innate penchant for magic and about her enchanted necklace. Neither of us had any idea how powerful she would become, and he never mentioned that she was searching for me. But you remember I told you about other people with knowledge of The Great Synergy and the impending war. We can add the mysterious Mrs. Case to that list."

"But how can we trust her?" implored Rome. "She tried to murder us!" He glared at Mrs. Case as she ignored the conversation apparently zoning in on her task.

"Let us use our gifts to determine the

severity of our situation, Young Master," replied Mr. Jones. "My instruments no onger see evidence of an entrance to the portal back there. I see no dark energies emitting from it nor attaching to your school master. I do believe this portal is inert. Do your dragon senses detect anything evil from her anymore?"

Rome frowned. Mr. Jones was right. Rome did not pick up the foul scent of The Void on her any longer. Maybe all was well after all. Julian, who clearly felt everything was safe, struck up an interrogatory conversation with the woman when she took a break from her sorcery.

"So, you were alive the whole time that thing was inside you?" asked Julian. "That's kinda creepy. What was it like? When did it happen?"

Mrs. Case chuckled. Her laugh caused everyone to relax a little except for Krysta who was watching Rome and Cecilia intensely. "It happened last summer when I flew over here to make arrangements for our study abroad program. I stayed in a quaint bed and breakfast for a week while I had meetings with the local legislature and educators during the day. A local historian recommended I check out the lake to get some relaxation. He said he camped out here many times as a child. He said the woods were full of wisdom, but also strange happenings. That was the day that the Nocturn took me as its host. It must have been drawn to my Talisman." Mr. Jones shot a curious look her way. "A couple days later, I returned to The United States where it must have picked up on Rome and Julian because it made me watch them feverishly."

"It was no joke," said Julian. "You really creeped us out a few times."

"I sincerely apologize," said Mrs. Case. "It was so strange. It was like the Nocturn made me do and say things I did not want to. I was like a marionette being pulled this way and that even though I was fully conscious and was aware my actions were wrong."

"That is quite alright," said Mr. Jones. "All of that is in the past. We have successfully made the Nocturn withdraw to The Void, and you may now go on about your life." He paused. "What ARE your plans, Mrs. Case?"

"Well," she started. "That is what Camela and I have been discussing while you guys were away. I am very enticed by the dynamic you boys have set up. You have two warriors bound by The

Great Synergy and a wielder of magic used as an advisor or teacher. If it is alright with Krysta, I would like to step into that role for the girls." She looked at Krysta. "I know you have been fighting the Darkbrands for a while now simply as a duo. I believe I would be a great asset to your faction."

Krysta broke her stare off from Rome. "As long as you promise not to hit me with any more of those wind blasts," she giggled. "I would love to have you onboard as a confederate, an educator, and a sister."

"Well said, fair Master," laughed Mr. Jones. "Well said, indeed. So it is settled then! We shall be a collection of six heroes strong."

"What do you mean, old man?" asked Julian. "We're joining forces?"

Mrs. Case spoke up. "I think it's a marvelous idea. But it doesn't make much sense geographically, does it? I guess I will have to appeal to Mr. Rider to allow the boys to study here in England instead."

"Prithee, what of your occupation, old lady?" inquired Camela without a hint of callousness.

Mrs. Case was stunned for a second. "Ummm. I will simply quit my job, and move here. Perhaps Mr. Jones and I can find work at a local library."

"I know the perfect place," stated Rome. "It's where Jules and I first met the girls." He locked eyes with Krysta. "I mean, where we first met our partners. And where they first became so special to us." Krysta blushed slightly. He looked back at Mr. Jones. "The girl's school has the biggest library I've ever seen. You guys should try to get jobs here." He looked down at the unconscious Cecilia. "Is she going to be alright?"

"She will be fine," assured Mrs. Case. "I'm nearly done with the spell. Allow me to finish up while you all decide our next course of action." Again, the principal began weaving her spell on Cecilia's mind.

"A seamless transition, Mrs. Case," declared Mr. Jones. "In fact, I traveled here for a couple reasons. I have limited time to give you this information as well, so let us get together and discuss my findings."

"What's up?" asked Julian fiddling with Pandora's Die.

"Well, there are a couple things I need to share with you," explained Mr. Jones. "The first is that I have been doing careful portal studying while back in The U.S.A. The behavior inside The Void has gotten stranger the last few days. The Darkbrands are most definitely preparing for something. Either that, or something has already happened, and they are reacting to it."

"What could it be?" asked Rome.

Before Mr. Jones could respond, Krysta approached him and reached for his glasses. "Are these how you see into the portals, Mr. Jones?" she inquired.

"Indeed they are, fair Master," he replied. He let her remove them from his face. "They were a gift from my former teacher, Mr. Smith. I'm not quite sure how they are able to do what they do, but I am very fortunate to have them. They allow me to monitor the portals, but this task does not come without consequence."

"Prithee, warlock," commented Camela. "The answer is simple. You wear a Talisman upon your nose."

"What?" cried Mr. Jones. "A Talisman?"

"Yes," said Krysta. "We have studied, read about, and learned about them in our book."

"What book?" asked Mr. Jones.

"Why, the Reemergence book my father gave me," replied Camela with an ounce of sass.

Camela quickly pulled her "Reemergence: The Great Synergy" book from her Incredible Hulk backpack and handed it to Mr. Jones. He reluctantly took it from her tiny hand and pushed his glasses up onto the bridge of his nose. He licked his thumb and enthusiastically flipped through the pages until he came to the part he was looking for. Then, with wide eyes, he read the following excerpt.

> **The Magic Mirror of Shalott**- The great Poet Laureate, Lord Alfred Tennyson wrote a ballad about a mirror that allowed the Lady of Shalott to look into it and see different scenes from Camelot. His fictional work was based on a real artifact that existed in King Arthur's treasure room. It was given magical properties long ago during the first war for Earth, and it allowed beings to look into The Void as an act of monitoring its activities. Sometime in the

past, it was shattered, and the pieces were passed down as heirlooms. Legend says that these fragments of the mirror can still be used to peer into The Void, but not even the bravest warriors will try.

"By the blades of Gilgamesh!" shouted Mr. Jones. "This is both extraordinary and perturbing news, indeed. I was completely unaware that there were Talismans other than the six elemental ones. This explains so many of the questions my teacher left with me, but it definitely convolutes our recent plans to move to England." Mr. Jones touched his fingers to his forehead as if deep in contemplation. "Could it be? No! That could not be possible." Mr. Jones paced in small semicircles. "No. He would not have that information. Or could he? No one could have predicted that!" Mr. Jones stopped and spoke to the onlookers. "Perhaps, if I let you in on my other tidbit of information it will explain why it is distressing to know that I am in possession of one of the Talismans. Oh, Great Green Goliath!"

Julian slammed his hands on the ground. "Oh, for the love of... Holy Chicken Man's toothbrush! By the fingernails of Teddy Roosevelt! Just spit it out, man!"

"Oh, Julian," laughed Mr. Jones. "Of course, you know that Chicken Man has no teeth and therefore no need for a toothbrush."

For the first time since Rome had met him, Julian was absolutely silent.

Chapter Nineteen

"So," began Mr. Jones.

"Since the possibility of new allies has arisen, I have been using the internets for exploratory purposes. My goal was to find any new information or actual warriors to fight for our cause. What I found was a contact in New York that claims to be a beacon of information about the Talismans. Ironically, he calls himself Beacon. He left me one message regarding the Darkbrand army, saying that he believes that the Darkbrands are attempting to gather all the Talismans they can find. Now, I do not know what for, but I do have three speculative guesses. My first thought on this is that we have already seen a rampant uptick in Darkbrand harassment. It would appear that they are making more moves than in the past, and they are returning to previously scoured areas like moths to a flame. It seems as though they are searching something out. Perhaps something is drawing them to these specific portals. Which leads me to my second thought. I believe the Talismans are their endgame.   They would want to harness the powers of these items to use for their own means of destruction. The Tyrant King has long been known for wanting to get his hands on the relics since they could obviously hinder his domination of the realm. I also recently surmised that since The Great Synergy requires the use of a Talisman, perhaps the Darkbrands are collecting these so that humanity and the dragons would not be able to perform this ritual. Thus leaving us without a defense system against invasion."

Krysta chimed in. "But, Mr. Jones, the exact number of dragons is completely unknown, unqualified, and untraceable. All I've ever known is my family, and they said we were the last of our kind. What if all of our possible allies are here with us?" She glanced at Rome. "What if all the dragons left on Earth are represented by Rome, myself, and no others?"

"It is a theory I have explored," lamented Mr. Jones. "However, I think we must follow this tip from Beacon and see how far the rabbit hole leads. My contact is quite interested in meeting with a delegate from our faction." He nodded towards Camela. "Your book describes many more Talismans that have not yet been accounted for.

Our enemy is attempting to collect them. I think we should do the same. Perhaps my friend in New York can point us in the direction of some or even has one himself."

"And what if it is an entrapment, sage?" asked Camela. "How wouldst we justify walking blindly into the waiting arms of Nocturns and Minotaurs? You said yourself the Darkbrands have facilitated a catalyst to their movements. My desire is to defend this realm, but I REFUSE to have Krysta and myself march up to the canon's mouth!"

Mrs. Case spoke up. "I can attest to Mr. Jones's second idea. I was possessed by that Nocturn because of my Talisman. I could feel the thing hunger for more power. It was clearly sent on a mission to obtain my heirloom. That must be why it was drawn to you boys as well. It craved Pandora's Die of Hope."

"If that is the case, then we are all in grave danger," said Mr. Jones.

"Why's that?" asked Julian flippantly flipping his die in the air.

"Because by my count," explained Mr. Jones, "we exhibit four Talismans between us. If the mystery associate in New York's data is correct, we may be the biggest target in the world for Darkbrand aggression. We could have the entire foundation of the Darkbrand army searching for us as we speak."

Julian fumbled his die which dropped to the ground landing on the number five. Instantaneously, a slingshot appeared next to it. Camela sighed deeply and squatted on the ground.

"What need have we of Talismans when we have my brother's formidable frippery?" she said. "He also can manifest brushwood and metal knickknacks for clipping paper."

"Oh yeah!" responded Julian. "Maybe your stupid pigtails will scare the Darkbrands back to The Void!"

"What good are you as an ally anyways?" retorted Camela. "You were unable to even perform The Great Synergy to its fullest potential! You and your pocket lighter dragon are liabilities in my eyes!"

"Oh yeah," snapped Julian. "Well, if it wasn't for Bruce Lee over there, I would smack you upside your obnoxious little head!"

"Enough," interrupted Rome. "It is true that we are severely overmatched and cannot trust this source. But what is our other option? Annihilation?" He turned to Mr. Jones. "We will meet with your contact. Jules and I will go alone if necessary to avoid capture of the whole team." Rome bent down to look Camela in her eyes. "You may be bound to Julian by blood, but what we share is more real than anything I have ever felt. And our desire to stave off the invasion is truer than any idea conceived by mankind. You know this is true because you share the same feeling with Krysta. Julian WILL go with me to represent us in New York. Perhaps it is best if you and Krysta remain here with the Talismans. You two have proven yourselves as worthy defenders, and if we are captured, you will remain our last line of defense. We have to explore all options, Lady Camela. No matter how fleeting they may seem."

Camela frowned and kicked a rock. "Wise words, dragon. Please forgive my insults."

"You are brave, courageous, and valiant," said Krysta touching Rome on his shoulder. "I beseech you to make it back to us alive and thank you for your selfless volunteering."

"You will require guidance," said Mrs. Case.

"I have experienced the darktouch of a Nocturn. I may embody the best advisor for this mission. Besides, I am vastly experienced at chaperoning."

Mr. Jones characteristically touched his chin. "Then, it is settled," he exclaimed. "I will travel to England to join the girls and find employment. I will reach out to Beacon and alert him of our hope to meet. I can send all the information I have to Julian's tablet, and you can leave urgently. Mrs. Case has the flexibility to travel back to The United States with Rome and Julian so she must escort them. Lady Camela can work on getting her father to continue financing the boys' stay here, and Krysta will guard the Frostshard. We are a united front though our paths will take us in different directions."

Rome walked into the middle of the group. He stuck his hand out and waited for the rest to join him. Krysta immediately placed her palm on his. She gave him a knowing smile and did her patented giggle.

"Though I will worry, fret, and deplore your absence, Rome, I do understand the need to further our exploration."

Julian placed his hand in next. "I'll follow

you brother. No matter the end. No matter the enemy. Through the never!"

Camela's puny palm found its way to the top of the juncture. "Tis for Camelot, after all." She looked to the mages. "What do you wait for, elders?"

"We must find the Talismans," said Mrs. Case. "The next few days will shed light on that which is unknown." She joined the circle.

Mr. Jones pushed his glasses onto his nose. "I've waited a lifetime to witness what I have seen thus far. What wonders we shall find next can only be imagined. I embrace them gladly, indeed, Young Master."

Rome looked to his compatriots and took in each of their faces. He made mental notes of how each one reacted to the others. He trusted this circle and all their abilities. What lay ahead was strange and mysterious, but he knew this group was full of hope. Just like the hope springing eternal from the die in Julian's pocket. They had defeated one of The Tyrant King's Minotaurs. They had exorcised and banished one of his Nocturns. Perhaps this ragtag group of ensorcelled warriors could keep The Tyrant King locked into The Void for another century. Perhaps they could protect the realm they called home. Perhaps they could influence the pages of perpetual history. But first, they would need to transport Cecilia back to the dormitories so she could bask in the Dreamweaver spell. And despite all their collective abilities, none of them had a car.

To Be Continued

Made in the USA
Monee, IL
11 February 2021